*Look wh...*
*about th...*

## About Julie Leto

"Leto's got the touch!"
—*Romantic Times BOOKreviews*

"She loves pushing the envelope,
and dances on the edge with the
sizzle and crackle of lightning."
—*The Best Reviews*

"Smart, sophisticated and sizzling
from start to finish."
—*A Romance Review*

## About Leslie Kelly

"Once again, Leslie Kelly provides readers
with a sexy, witty, romantic and all-around
fun story to read."
—*Romance Reviews Today* on *Heated Rush*

"*Don't Open Till Christmas* is a present in itself
where the humor and the sizzling sex never stop.
Top Pick!"
—*Romantic Times BOOKreviews*

"Oh, this one is definitely wild,
but even better, it also aims for the heart."
—*Mrs. Giggles* on *One Wild Wedding Night*

## ABOUT THE AUTHORS

Harlequin Blaze has been a perennial home for *New York Times* and *USA TODAY* bestselling author **Julie Leto** and her ultra-sexy, yet romantic stories of powerful men and the women with the strength and moxie to tame them. With more than thirty novels to her credit, Julie has been recognized with such awards as a *Romantic Times BOOKreviews* Best Blaze for her 2007 release *Stripped,* and she was nominated for a RITA® Award for her novella "Surrender." She shares a popular blog, www.plotmonkeys.com, with her best friends, Carly Phillips, Janelle Denison and Leslie Kelly—with whom she also shares this collection. For more information about her upcoming releases and to win great prizes, stop by the jungle!

**Leslie Kelly** is an award-winning author of more than thirty Harlequin novels. A three-time nominee for the highest award in romantic fiction, the RWA RITA® Award, she is also a National Reader's Choice Award winner and has received a *Romantic Times BOOKreviews* Award. Leslie lives in Maryland with her husband and three daughters. To learn more about her writing, please visit www.lesliekelly.com or her blog site, www.plotmonkeys.com.

New York Times Bestselling Author

# Julie Leto
# Leslie Kelly

## MORE BLAZING
## BEDTIME STORIES

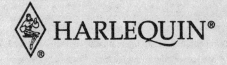

HARLEQUIN®

TORONTO • NEW YORK • LONDON
AMSTERDAM • PARIS • SYDNEY • HAMBURG
STOCKHOLM • ATHENS • TOKYO • MILAN • MADRID
PRAGUE • WARSAW • BUDAPEST • AUCKLAND

Recycling programs
for this product may
not exist in your area.

ISBN-13: 978-0-373-79505-5

MORE BLAZING BEDTIME STORIES
Copyright © 2009 by Harlequin Books S.A.

The publisher acknowledges the copyright holders of the
individual works as follows:

INTO THE WOODS
Copyright © 2009 by Julie Leto

ONCE UPON A MATTRESS
Copyright © 2009 by Leslie Kelly

# CONTENTS

# INTO THE WOODS
## Julie Leto

To Leslie Kelly—thank you for opening the portal into Elatyria and allowing me to play in your world! Even without the "f." ☺

# Prologue

*In the enchanted land of Elatyria...*

ONCE UPON A TIME, Tatiana Starlingham believed she was destined to be a princess.

She was, after all, the seventh and youngest daughter of the wealthiest merchant in the land. As her sisters were each more beautiful than the last, every one, including Tatiana, had been courted by none but the most eligible princes. Heirs from the surrounding kingdoms lavished the Starlingham daughters with jewels and furs and priceless gifts. Girls from peasants to princesses wished to have been born into the Starlingham household.

So it wasn't surprising that on the day after her sixth sister's marriage, Tatiana answered the summons to her parents' salon, fully expecting to learn that a gorgeous, kind and wealthy man of noble birth wished to make her his bride.

When she entered the room at dawn, sunlight streamed through the many glittering windows. She blinked against the brightness, but strolled in with grace and measured steps, eyes dutifully averted, aware that her intended groom might be waiting beside her father right now. She had flirted with several interesting prospects at the reception the night before. Prince Michael had incredible green eyes and when he'd realized how well she understood the importance of well-bred horses to an effective infantry, he'd nearly fallen to one knee on the spot. Prince Dennis, while not quite as tall as she'd have liked, had spent nearly a quarter of an hour crowing about how his mother's sapphire choker would glisten against

Tatiana's appropriately pale skin. And Prince Lyle! He'd actually sought her advice on a tricky truce negotiation with a warlord from his kingdom who lived on the border of Tatiana's father's most profitable trade route.

Tatiana, you see, was not like her sisters. She did not intend to marry the first prince who asked. Like all the Starlingham daughters, she had been blessed with unsurpassed beauty, but Tatiana had also been gifted with brains, tact and cunning. While her sisters had ignored their tutors to try on new gowns or experiment with the latest hairstyles, Tatiana had studied. Her greatest ambition—to become a princess—was merely a stepping stone to her coronation as a queen.

After a deep curtsy to her parents, she looked up, only slightly surprised to see not a prostrate prince, but a woman standing beside her father. Or rather, floating. Tiny wings flittered behind her, elevating her delicate slippers a foot above the ground. The woman was lovely, but had a keen look in her eyes—one that made Tatiana quiver.

"Father? Mother?"

"Sit down, Tatiana," her mother said, an extra dose of regal in her tone.

Tatiana noticed immediately that her father would not look her in the eye.

She curtsied again, but remained on her feet. "Who is this woman?"

A corner of the woman's mouth curved upward. "Headstrong, this one. Good. She'll need to be stubborn to fill my shoes."

Tatiana glanced at the floating slippers. "Father, what does she mean?"

"This is Romilda, the fairy godmother to the kingdoms," her mother introduced.

Had the atmosphere not been so fraught with tension and foreboding, Tatiana might have been excited at meeting a fairy godmother. The main duty of such women was to arrange love matches that benefited a young lady's heart. But there was something about this Romilda's shrewd stare that made Tatiana believe the fairy had something else in mind for her—something that did not include a lucrative engagement.

Before she could say another word, Romilda floated to her, hovered for a second, then flew in a circle, checking her out from head to toe. She must be prowling on behalf of an extremely powerful prince if she was inspecting Tatiana so carefully.

"Do you like what you see?" Tatiana asked.

The godmother snorted. "Never quite learned that don't-speak-until-you're-spoken-to rule, did you?"

"That is for children."

"And princesses," the godmother contradicted. "No man likes a mouthy woman."

Tatiana watched her parents exchange an uneasy look.

"My prince will have to be more tolerant, then," Tatiana replied.

"Your prince?" The godmother laughed, the echo ringing as she glided back to her place beside Tatiana's parents. "Haven't you told her? And I thought magical creatures such as myself were the cruelest in the land. To keep your daughter in the dark about our bargain—"

Tatiana's blood chilled. "What bargain?"

The fairy godmother zipped toward her and instantly, Tatiana's mouth dried. The woman's eyes were cold and calculating. Tatiana's father still would not look at her and her mother sat, back ramrod-straight, as if in a trance.

"I should let them tell you," Romilda said. "But let me ask you a question which may lead you to the answer on your own. Why is your father so wealthy?"

Tatiana looked to the man she'd revered her entire life with a hopeful glance, but still, he would not meet her gaze. "He's a brilliant merchant. He's found the means to trade peacefully with all the kingdoms and stay out of their wars."

"Has he always struck you as a smart man?"

Tatiana's heart dropped into the pit of her stomach. Her father was easy with a laugh, kind and indulgent, but she was old enough now to know that he wasn't exactly the brightest flame in the candelabra.

"Why do you ask?"

Only Tatiana could hear Romilda's surprisingly girlish giggle. "Apparently, you are both diplomatic and smart, girl. Good. That will serve you well."

"How?"

"Fairy godmothers have to be sharp-witted, discreet and tactful. You'll be arranging matches that will affect the political future of the kingdoms."

Tatiana swallowed, but found her throat had swelled with fear. Her entire life, she'd dreamed of taking her place within the political hierarchy of the kingdoms by becoming a queen. To rule. To command. Her aspirations soared above those of her simpleton sisters. How could she now be destined to serve them?

"I'm the daughter of an influential merchant," Tatiana insisted, finding her voice. "I am destined to be a—"

"Queen," Romilda finished. "Yes, yes. You do dream big. You would have been a pleasure to place. But your ambitions are, I'm afraid, the ultimate irony. And the price you must pay for your parents' greed. Your mother was a princess once, did you know that?"

Tatiana's eyes widened. She'd always perceived her mother as distant and haughty, but she was of royal blood?

The fairy godmother pretended to frown, but the light of a nasty smile sparkled in her eyes. "Forty years ago, her father was deposed in a terrible war, spawned when she married her footman, your father, for love. She ignored my advice to marry a prince to ensure peace in her kingdom. Then, a year later, she called me, begging me to save her from abject poverty, to make her new husband rich and give her beautiful daughters she could marry off to princes and continue her regal bloodlines."

Tatiana gasped when her mother—always so proud, always so perfect—dropped her humiliated gaze to her lap.

"I made a bargain with her," Romilda continued. "In

exchange for seven daughters of untold beauty and wealth normally afforded only to those of royal blood, I wanted a way out of my servitude as a fairy godmother."

"Servitude?"

"You don't think we're born like this, do you? We're not exactly compact size and living in flower gardens or tree hollows. Fairy godmothers are made, dear. We're like genies in a bottle, enslaved to our magical purpose. Unless we find someone desperate enough to free us."

Her greedy eyes darted to Tatiana's mother.

"And my mother can help you gain your freedom? How?"

The fairy's lip curled into a snarl. "By promising me that her youngest daughter would be my replacement."

And it was at that moment that Tatiana Starlingham, for the first and last time in her life, fainted to the floor.

# *1*

*Four centuries later...*

SHE WAS going to kill that elf.

Her feet hurt. Her cloak was snagged and torn by brambles. Her wings itched. Still, she pressed onward, her wand out of sight but at the ready in case Rumplestiltskin's no-good, great-great grandson had lied when he'd pointed her down the path to her emancipation. The chasm between her world and the next—the so called "real world"—had to be around here someplace. Tatiana had to find the doorway tonight or she'd go mad. If she had to listen to yet another vapid, airheaded princess sing another saccharine aria listing all the impossible qualities Tatiana should find in the "prince of her dreams," she was going to puke a rainbow.

She stumbled in a divot on the uneven ground, caught herself, cursed, then looked over her shoulder at the land behind her. In the far distance, sparks of the golden glow that hovered above her homeland defied the darkness. At one time, she'd thought the place remarkably beautiful—enchanting and full of promise and possibility. Just like her. Four hundred years later, she could hardly picture the girl who'd mused about marrying a prince in order to ascend to the throne.

She had no trouble, however, remembering exactly what she'd felt like that fateful morning when her parents had turned her over to the fairies. And for four centuries, she'd served dutifully. Thanks to her, every one of her nieces had married well, even if she'd had to pawn a few of the less-bright ones off on dukes and earls. And she'd found loyal young ladies for all her nephews. She'd worked her magic for their daughters and sons, and *their* daughters and sons. Nowadays, some weren't so adamant about marrying only for royal blood or political gain. A few had actually opted to wed for love—and without selling out any of their children in the process.

Not that Tatiana understood the concept of love. As part of a fairy godmother's bargain, her ability to experience romantic emotions like desire, lust or heartbreak had been magically suppressed. But while she couldn't understand the instantaneous spark her charges often sang about, she did find the physical expression of those feelings rather interesting to watch.

There was no rule in the fairy godmother Book of Decrees that said she couldn't learn a few things by observation, but that she'd been reduced to voyeurism did not sit well with her.

After spending more generations than she could count as a spectator, Tatiana was ready to play the game. She'd spent four centuries matchmaking and saving mostly doormat divas from servitude to wicked stepmothers and upstart trolls (or otherwise ill-tempered royal playboys) and Tatiana had had enough. According to Joe Stiltskin, Rumple's equally dodgy progeny, she had only one way out.

Time had not erased her disgust over the bargain her mother had made. Tatiana wasn't about to hoist this job off on some other unsuspecting girl with tiaras in her eyes. No, she was going to get out of the fairy godmother business the only *other* way that existed—she was going to cross over into the human world and grant the wishes of the first young woman she met.

And she was going to do it without magic.

Because if she could accomplish this task before the next full moon, she'd be transformed into a human herself and would never again have to hear the impossible dreams of another bubbleheaded bride-to-be.

Above her, the moon emerged from behind a blanket of thick, dark clouds. A chill spiked through the cloak and the ground suddenly seemed both rockier and loamier. She closed her eyes tightly, spoke a spell that might have ensured her safety in the world of her birth, then stepped into the dense trees that were the boundary into the human realm.

She stopped twenty paces in and looked around. Other than the fact that it was darker than a witch's soul, she felt no difference. She marched another ten paces into the forest, slapping aside low-hanging branches that in any other forest she'd accuse of trying to cop a feel. The cloak shifted, hanging heavier on her shoulders and the stab in her side from her wand disappeared. The woods were eerily silent—as if no one existed to hear even the whispering whirl of the wind.

She walked for what seemed like an hour until finally, she heard something.

Crying.

Definitely feminine and definitely distraught.

Tatiana smiled. If there was one sound that was music to a fairy godmother's ears, it was a young girl in misery.

Girls in misery always had wishes they needed granted.

Tatiana hurried forward, stopping short when the same voice started cursing.

"That's an awful lot of crusty language coming from a girl your age," Tatiana said once she found the little slip of a thing stalking around a break in the trees, shaking her fist at the sky.

The girl screamed and turned to run, but Tatiana snagged her by the sleeve of her oversized jacket.

"Who'd you get this from, a giant?" she asked, enjoying the feel of the well-worn leather beneath her fingers. The sensation was surprising. She'd felt plenty of saddles and boots and even a few princely doublets in her time, but none had evoked such an instant warmth.

"It's…my…stupid…brother's," the girl answered, tugging hard against Tatiana's hold with each word.

Tatiana released her, which, of course, sent the chippy flying to the ground.

The girl scrambled away from Tatiana like an overturned crab. "Who are you?"

"My name is Tatiana," she said, crossing her arms. "And you are?"

"Harper," she answered, sniffing and wiping her running nose on her hand.

Ew.

Tatiana waved her hand to produce a handkerchief, but alas, her magic, as Joe had predicted, was gone. Well, that was damned inconvenient. She dug into the pockets of the borrowed cloak and found a wrinkled bandana that smelled vaguely of damp straw. She handed it to Harper and once the girl was sufficiently blown and wiped, extended her hand to help her to her feet.

"I'm not going to hurt you," Tatiana said.

"As if you could," Harper shot back.

Tatiana ignored the child's bravado.

"What's a girl like you doing in a place like this?"

Harper smirked. "Isn't that some kind of old-fashioned pick-up line? You're not a lesbo, are you?"

Tatiana blinked. "You do speak English here?"

"Last time I checked," the teen replied.

"Good," Tatiana said with a sigh. "I know German and French, but I'm a little rusty. So, let's go back to my first question. What is a pretty young thing like you doing out in the forest in the middle of the night?"

"It's not a forest. It's a swamp."

Tatiana gave the air a tentative sniff. "Is that what that smell is?"

"Hey," Harper protested. "This is my home, okay? It's really cool, once you get used to it."

Tatiana eyed the girl suspiciously. She had that whininess in her voice that Tatiana knew too well—the sound of someone trying to convince herself that she liked something better than she actually did.

"Okay, the swamp is…cool," Tatiana agreed, though in her estimation, the temperature was well beyond comfortable and more akin to sultry. "So explain why you were crying."

Harper swiped the residual moisture from her face. "I wasn't—"

"All right, all right," Tatiana conceded, not exactly thrilled with how this was progressing. The girl was inordinately argumentative. And yet, she liked her. "You weren't crying. But you were pretty angry, you can't deny that. So why don't you tell me what I can do to help."

"Why?"

"Excuse me?"

"Why are you going to help? I don't know you. What are you doing here, anyway?"

Tatiana rolled her eyes. Argumentative and inquisitive. She suddenly—and briefly—missed the self-absorbed princesses who accepted her magical presence without questions, told her what they wanted and let her get to work.

"I'm lost," Tatiana answered.

"Oh," the teen replied. Obviously, this answer satisfied her. "That doesn't explain why you want to help me."

"Have you heard of quid pro quo?"

"It's Latin for '*something for something.*'"

Tatiana raised an eyebrow.

"My stupid, idiotic, overbearing, asshole of a brother makes me study Latin," Harper explained.

Ah-ha. Tatiana now guessed that said brother was the cause of the girl's misery. But before she set off to right filial wrongs and ensure her freedom from fairy godmotherhood, she'd need the girl's cooperation.

"Well, if you know what it means, you understand why I want to help you. I solve whatever problem has you so angry and you show me the way out of your swamp."

Harper wiped her nose with the bandanna again. "You can't help."

"You don't know that. Just tell me what you need," Tatiana encouraged. "I promise I'll do everything in my power to make your wishes come true."

# 2

JACK ST. CLOUD slammed the door to his sister's room and bellowed for Mrs. Bradley. The cook and housekeeper took a full five minutes to respond, during which time he'd searched Harper's room twice more, called her cell phone and sent her a text message. He was halfway down the stairs when the woman finally rounded the corner, her gray curls webbed by a hairnet and her bathrobe untied at her waist.

"Yes, Mr. St. Cloud?"

He stopped, inhaled and forced his words out slowly and calmly.

"Where is Harper?"

Mrs. Bradley leaned to the side, as if she somehow expected to see the teenager hiding behind him. An ex-pro football player, Jack could indeed shield someone as petite as his sister. If only protecting her was that easy. Only two hours ago, the fourteen-year-old brat had screamed, stamped her feet and pounded her fists on his chest when he'd forbidden her even to think about throwing herself into the sharp teeth and merciless cogs of the New York City theater machine. Which was why, he guessed, she'd run away.

"She's not in her room?" Mrs. Bradley inquired.

Jack willed himself to remain calm. Four years ago, when Harper had turned ten and developed a penchant for playing her stereo at eardrum-destroying decibels, both Mrs. Bradley and Harper had begged—no, pleaded—for privacy. Reluctantly, he'd allowed the housekeeper to move out of the adjoining bedroom where the older woman, who'd acted as a nanny, had lived since Jack took over Harper's guardianship when she was two. Now, he regretted that decision very much.

"If she were in her room, would I have called you?" he asked.

"Did you check her studio, sir? She puts those head-phones on and turns up the volume and you could scream yourself hoarse—"

"I checked."

Another concession he'd made in his quest to keep Harper happy—turning Mrs. Bradley's old room into a music studio. He'd thought buying his sister all the latest in sound and video technology would quell her insatiable desire to run off to New York and become the next big Broadway star. Potential speculation in the gossip rags flashed across his mind. *Harper St. Cloud, ingénue daughter of the famous (and now quite dead) Marina St. Cloud, debuts on the Great White Way. Will the sky be the limit for this St. Cloud? Will the bright bulbs of Broadway burn her out like they did her mother? Will her brother's sacrifice of a championship NFL career to care for his orphaned sister turn out to be a complete waste of time and talent?*

Okay, Jack doubted Page Six would care much about his football aspirations, but damn it, he cared. He had not quit at the height of his profession just to watch his sister get fried to a crisp the way their mother had been. He'd promised himself as much after their mother's suicide. With their father already dead from a heart attack at forty, he'd had no choice.

Now that Harper was missing, Jack might suffer the same fate as his parents. Though his heart was slamming against his chest, he was in perfect physical shape. Mentally? That was up in the air when Harper got into one of her moods.

The wily little pain in the ass had put the equipment he'd bought her to good use all right. She'd created an audition tape for Broadway producers who now wanted to meet her in person. Only four hours ago, they'd called to seek Jack's permission for his minor sister to try out for the part of Cinderella in a revival of Rogers and Hammerstein's titular work. He, of course, had said no.

She'd claimed she was adult enough to audition.

He'd forbidden it.

She'd insisted that this was the role she was born for and that if he didn't let her try out, her entire future would be just as sad and empty as his.

He'd unplugged her phone, disconnected her stereo and grounded her for two weeks.

And now she was missing.

"I'm sure she's just gone out to cool off," Mrs. Bradley said calmly. "This isn't the first time she's run into the bayou for some peace and quiet after you two had a row. I'll turn on the outdoor lights and get dressed."

Damn, damn and triple damn.

"No," Jack said. He walked down two stairs, sat, and shoved his hands through his hair. "I'm sorry, Mrs. Bradley. I shouldn't have woken you. Harper is my problem, not yours."

The older woman crossed her arms over her chest. "Well, she is that, sir. *Your* problem, I mean. Because with everyone else in the world, she seems to get on just fine."

"That's because everyone else gives her what she wants."

"She's charming," Mrs. Bradley said. "Like her mother."

"Which is precisely why I have to put limits on her."

With a weary sigh, he stood, stretched out his long legs and tugged at his sweatpants. "Please hit the spotlights," he asked the housekeeper. "Then go back to bed. I'll find her."

"Try the boathouse first," Mrs. Bradley suggested before breezing off toward the kitchen.

Despite the inherent dangers of living in the middle of nowhere, Mrs. Bradley was right to be relatively unconcerned. Once the location of an old hunting cabin built by their great-grandfather, this land was in their blood. After becoming Harper's guardian, Jack could think of no better place to live to protect his sister from the swarms of people anxious to exploit the tragic little heiress foisted on a brother who had no idea how to raise a kid.

But at least he'd made sure that Harper could navigate the

acreage around the bayou as easily as she could her bedroom, which, with piles of clothes, books, CDs, the occasional half-eaten box of Cap'n Crunch with Crunch Berries, and mounds of various teenage-girl detritus, could prove just as perilous.

As he turned to his wing of the house, the walls of windows that made up the entire first floor gleamed with bright white light. Anyone within a mile radius would think it was noon and not two o'clock in the morning.

He grabbed a faded workout jacket from the peg in his bathroom and slipped into it, not bothering to zip it up. The night air was the same as the day air—hot. He gave a cursory glance to his own private studio and, noticing the door open, went back in and closed it. He'd indulged Harper's need for her sanctuary because he had one, as well. And since there were just some things a teenage girl didn't need to know about her brother, he locked the door before heading out into the night.

"HOLY ILLUMINATED Night Parade," Tatiana said, squinting her eyes against the glare pouring from the direction where Harper insisted her house was. "Does Walt know your brother stole his idea?"

"Walt Disney? He's dead."

Tatiana stopped walking. "I thought I hadn't seen him in a while."

"What?" Harper asked.

Tatiana cleared her throat. It wasn't exactly common knowledge that authors like the brothers Grimm and creators like Walt Disney had made regular visits to Elatyria, which was why she wasn't entirely disconcerted about how things operated here. She hadn't been updated in a while, but she'd get the gist.

"That is one serious night-light your brother has," Tatiana said, changing the direction of the conversation. "Did someone lock him in a closet as a child or something?"

Harper snorted. "Jack isn't afraid of the dark. He isn't afraid of anything."

It was Tatiana's turn to sniff derisively. "He's a man, isn't he? They're all afraid of something. Dragons. Peasant revolts. Women who require fidelity. The list goes on and on."

Harper did not look up. "You don't know Jack. Slaying a dragon would be a piece of cake. He played pro football. He's no wuss."

"Maybe not, but I'm sure there's something that keeps him up at night."

Harper dug her hands deep into the pockets of her jeans. "The only thing that spooks my brother is not living up to his responsibility."

She said the last word with mock derision, but Tatiana had been around one too many spoiled young girls to fall for that.

"Responsibility isn't a bad thing," she reasoned. "Once you understand his fear, however, you'll be able to find the best way around it."

"You seem awfully sure of yourself," Harper said, her doubt clear.

"Watch and learn," Tatiana said, though under her breath.

On their walk back to the house, Tatiana had listened while Harper explained what had caused her fight with her older brother and guardian. Not everything she said made sense, but Tatiana was pretty good at faking things—as evidenced by the countless times she'd convinced intelligence-challenged princesses that she actually cared if they got their happily-ever-afters.

But with Harper, she really did care. She was a little surprised by this, as much as she was by the kid herself. Harper might only be fourteen years old, but she had a smart mouth and an old soul. She wanted desperately to go to this Broadway place and sing. She had a group of powerful people called "producers" who wanted to hear her just as urgently. Unfortunately, her brother was standing in her way.

"Jack's okay, except when he's keeping me from pursuing

my dream. He already lived his," Harper said with a whine that could only be perfected by someone who had not reached adulthood. "It's my turn."

Before they stepped through a break in the trees that would spill them onto the expansive lawn in front of Jack St. Cloud's bayou home, Tatiana took Harper's arm. Tatiana had been lucky to find Harper St. Cloud on her first night in the "other" world. She couldn't waste her one shot at freedom. Spells and magical bargains were full of loopholes and tricky clauses. If she wanted out of the fairy-godmother business—which she did—she had to do this right.

"Make your wishes."

"What?"

Tatiana instinctively reached for her wand, but it wasn't there. She blew out a quick breath, remembering she had to fulfill Harper's dreams without the use of magic. By the next full moon. If she failed, she'd be stuck as a fairy godmother for all of eternity.

"I could have been lost in the bayou for days if I hadn't found you," she said as preamble. Joe Stiltskin hadn't said she had to keep her situation a secret from the girl whose wish she would fulfill, but somehow, Tatiana didn't think Harper would cooperate with a stranger if she rattled on about her former occupation. "I owe you my life. Tell me precisely what you wish to happen when we confront your brother and I'll do whatever I can to make sure your wishes come true."

Harper didn't hesitate. "I wish to sing on Broadway," she said enthusiastically, then she grabbed Tatiana's hands and tugged her close. "And I want to do it with Jack's approval."

Tricky as a troll, this one. Tatiana narrowed her eyes, but grinned at the hopefulness in Harper's voice. "Okay, then. Let's meet Jack St. Cloud and convince him to give us both exactly what we want."

## 3

"'FEE, fie, foe, fum, I smell the blood of an Englishman. Be he alive or be he dead… Should I grind his bones, or get him in my bed?'" Tatiana whispered, her insides liquefying at the sight of Jack St. Cloud vaulting from the porch to the lawn. The ground shook, though whether the effect was literal or figurative, she wasn't sure.

Yelling behind him for someone named Mrs. Bradley to douse the overpowering lights, Jack marched across the expansive lawn with strong, measured steps, like a man who could crush a mountain with his heel. The lights flicked off except for twin golden globes at the top of the porch. The blinding effects of sudden shadows lasted until he stood directly in front of them.

Like his mansion on stilts in the midst of the bayou, Jack St. Cloud towered over them. His hair was thick and long, the ends sweeping over shoulders that seemed to be chiseled from the same stone as his square jaw. His pants, made from some magical material that clung to every impressive curve and bulge, emphasized the muscles on his thighs and slim, tapered hips. His unzipped jacket revealed pecs and abs she couldn't tear her gaze from.

Walt's disciples might have borrowed from her universe to create characters like the book-loving Belle, but for the brute, Gaston, they'd clearly looked no further than Jack St. Cloud.

"Explain," he demanded of his sister.

His voice rumbled over the silent yard and for the first time in four hundred years, Tatiana knew the heated, weakening effects of lust. Her center core compressed into a pointed spike that drove straight down through her pelvis. She blinked, suddenly aware of his gaze raking down her body.

Instinctively, she pulled the cloak closer.

"And who the hell are you?" he snapped.

Bravely, Tatiana thought, Harper stepped in front of her. "This is…Ana. She was lost in the bayou and I found her."

His eyes narrowed suspiciously. "What were you doing out here in the middle of the night?"

The question was for Tatiana, not Harper.

"She got dumped," Harper replied. "By some asshole 'cause she wouldn't put out."

"Can't she speak for herself?"

Jack's volume dropped, but his gentler tone was even more dangerous.

Tatiana cleared her throat. "Of course I can. I'm just—"

Harper tossed Tatiana a cautious look over her shoulder, reminding her to stick to the cover story they'd devised on their way to the house. The girl was clever. Of course, the fact that this talented, manipulative and bright girl hadn't yet come up with a way to convince her brother to give her what she wanted did not bode well for Tatiana's chances at success.

"I'm shaken up," she continued, trying her best to look at least slightly simpering. She'd certainly witnessed the emotion enough times. "I went to a ball—an event—with the brother of a friend and on our way home, he said he knew a short cut. Suddenly, we were in the bayou and his hands were everywhere and I just got out and—"

As Harper had predicted, Jack's eyes instantly softened, and he held out his hand in welcome. White-knight syndrome. She'd seen it a million times. Usually in knights.

"Bastard," Jack said. "Are you all right? Do you need to call someone?"

She forced herself to look rattled, but resilient. "I'm fine, now that Harper found me. I'm not accustomed to this…

environment. There's no telling what might have happened if your sister hadn't heard me crying and come running."

For emphasis, she shivered visibly, then nearly lost her ability to breathe when Jack shrugged out of his jacket and slipped it around her shoulders. "Let's get you inside. Both of you."

He might have thrown a derisive glare at his sister, but Tatiana was too overwhelmed to notice. Masculine and musky and so heady she feared she might fall into a swoon worthy of a pin-prick on a spinning wheel, his scent put the rest of her senses on instant alert. Suddenly, it wasn't so dark outside. The grass beneath her feet seemed soft enough for her to float over even without her wings and her mouth watered for a taste of something…anything…that might be lingering on Jack St. Cloud's lips.

Suddenly, she understood those princesses more than she ever had before. This love-at-first-sight phenomenon was powerful stuff. Luckily, Tatiana had been around the kingdom enough times to know this wasn't love. It was attraction. Sexual awareness. Lust, pure and simple.

And it was divine.

He looked down at her, concern etching his bone-melting features. "You sure you're okay?"

"No," Harper interjected. "I think she needs to stay the night. She's really upset. She can have my room. I'll sleep on the couch."

"If we put her in your room, we might never find her again," Jack quipped. "The guest room is a mess, too. She can have my bed for the night."

With him in it?

She could only hope.

After the friendly housekeeper named Mrs. Bradley made tea, Jack had Harper find something for Tatiana to wear. Harper returned with what looked like half a night gown. Tatiana accepted the sleepwear and then followed Harper upstairs, more than a tad disappointed that Jack hadn't wanted to tuck her in himself.

"Here it is." Harper swung open double doors that led to the master suite. "The inner sanctum."

She flicked a switch near the door. A soft blue glow flared as if sapphire lights were hidden beneath the sleek crown molding. Tatiana instantly focused on the bed, which was twice as long as she'd ever seen and just as wide. The bedclothes were a deep midnight blue. The collection of pillows in white and gold reminded her of stars in the sky. The decor was sparse and modern and deeply human. She'd never find a place like this on her side of the woods.

"Wow," she said.

"Pretty boring, I know," Harper said.

"No," Tatiana argued instantly. "I mean, it's a little cold, I guess, and it's so…well, neat."

And sensual, in a minimalist way.

"As I said, boring," Harper concluded.

Harper took the jacket from around Tatiana's shoulders. Instantly, she missed Jack's scent, especially when she caught a whiff of the cloak underneath. She discarded the motheaten covering she'd borrowed from Joe Stiltskin in a corner near the door, then looked down at her gown, which sparkled azure in the eerie blue lights of Jack's room.

"That's beautiful," Harper said, fingering the beadwork on Tatiana's sleeves.

She'd been wearing this dress—or similar versions—for over four centuries. The thought of taking it off thrilled her to no end.

"There are stays in the back. Can you—?"

Harper got immediately to work. "How'd you get in this thing, anyway?"

"A maid," she replied.

"You have a maid? Are you rich? Because we are, in case you haven't noticed."

Tatiana scanned the room, noting the short columns topped with sculpture and original paintings on the walls. "I noticed. And your brother made all this from playing a sport?"

"Not all of it," Harper said, struggling with a stay that had obviously been knotted a few decades too long. "My dad was a Broadway producer. And my mother was a stage star. They left us everything when they died. Did I say 'us'? What a crock. I don't see a penny until I turn twenty-five. Jack now rules my trust fund, but he used to be a cornerback for the New York Giants."

Tatiana swallowed a chuckle. "He is a giant."

"He's a big guy," Harper conceded. "Anyway, what else is there to do around here? Make more money and exercise. It's all he does."

"That's *all?*"

Harper shrugged.

Tatiana frowned, then unbidden, yawned. She was exhausted—and the prospect of slipping into Jack's sheets and enveloping herself in his scent again made her dizzy with anticipation.

"Well, you're going to have to tell me more about him if our plan to facilitate your audition is going to work."

Harper matched Tatiana's yawn with a wide maw of her own. "In the morning, 'kay? I'm beat."

And with that, the kid left.

Tatiana tugged the sleeves of her dress, then stepped out of the lace, tulle and silk of her standard-issue fairy godmother gown. Now that she'd left Elatyria, she'd lost her effervescent glow—that extra "sparkle" that made fairy godmothers appear much more beautiful than they actually were. Worried about the aftereffects, she stepped in front of the closest mirror.

Her hair had fallen out of the careful curls that had once twined around her tiara—only her tiara was gone, leaving her hair a mass of tangles. Dirt smudged her nose and cheeks and her lips looked especially pink and swollen. She turned to find a basin to wash in when her gaze drifted lower, to her breasts.

Wow. She had really great tits.

Funny how she'd never noticed before.

She circled the globes of flesh with her hands and a spark

of sensation struck her. Her nipples extended and she couldn't resist running her fingers over them, gasping when twin jolts of excitement shot straight through her skin.

She did it again, marveling at how a sizzle of warmth speared between her legs each time she touched herself. This wasn't lust—it was arousal. Sweet, torturous and mind-numbing. She continued to pluck at her nipples mercilessly, her breath catching with each spiral of pleasure when she heard a soft knock behind her.

She spun, her hands instinctively covering herself.

"Harper?"

The door opened an inch. "No, it's Jack."

## 4

SINCE he'd installed the ultra-thick doors on his bedroom himself, Jack knew that Ana Starling, or whatever his sister had said her name was, wouldn't hear him knock unless he opened the door a crack. He'd had no idea that the thin sliver of space was enough for him to spot her standing beside his dresser wearing nothing but pale panties.

He stepped back, but the image of her breasts—plump and pale and centered with dark, erect nipples—burned into his brain like ignited flash powder. The fire quickly blazed down to the areas of his anatomy that had been long ignored.

She was a guest. She was a friend, however new, of his little sister. And he'd nearly walked in on her while she…what? He didn't want to think about it. Well, actually, he did. But he didn't think his neglected libido could stand it.

He cleared his throat, hoping his voice wouldn't sound as strangled as his insides.

"Are you decent?" he asked, closing his eyes and hoping she'd buy his implication that he hadn't seen anything.

"Wh-what?"

"Are you dressed?" he said, more loudly. "I need to grab a few things."

Again, he pictured her totally *grab*-worthy breasts. He cursed quietly, then tried to come up with something to say that didn't contain a lusty double entendre. He settled on, "I need to gather a few belongings."

"Just a moment, please."

With his eyes shut tight, he found himself fantasizing about her dashing across the room, those lovely, pale breasts bouncing, her slim stomach fluttering, her round ass curved in offering as she bent to retrieve her dress. He'd only caught a quick view of her erect nipples, but his brain had registered the precise size and shape with the same accuracy he used to calculate exchange rates and predict the yo-yo movements of the Dow Jones. He would never have imagined she was so shapely underneath that horrible, smelly cloak. Now, he doubted he'd erase the picture of her luscious, naked body from his memory—ever. Good thing she was leaving in the morning.

"O-okay. You can come in now."

He opened the door, expecting to see her back in her cloak, but his lungs seized when he saw how she'd wrapped herself in his jacket. *Only* his jacket. The hem reached almost to her knees, but the distinctive curve of her hips would not be hidden, nor would the generous helping of cleavage peeking out from the loosened zipper. Any other woman might have looked like a gray mushroom in his oversized hoodie, but somehow Ana Starling looked more like a stone that, if polished with precision, would become a priceless gem.

"I'm sorry," he apologized as he entered, trying to keep his mind focused only on the supplies he needed. *iPod. Toothbrush. Book. iPod. Toothbrush. Book. iPod. Toothbrush.*

*Condom.*

"No," he muttered.

"Excuse me?"

"Nothing," he said, grabbing a small overnight bag from the bathroom closet. He shoved his personal items inside, leaving the condoms in the back of the medicine cabinet where they belonged.

"Oh," she said, sounding slightly disappointed.

He chanced a quick glance into the bedroom. She seemed to be holding the fabric of his jacket up to her nose. Had he washed it since his last workout?

"I hope you're comfortable," he said. "You can take a shower in here or whatever. Not now," he said, just in case she misinterpreted his invitation. "After I get out of your way. And if you need anything, there's an intercom beside the bed. I'll be able to—"

"An intercom?"

Her intense curiosity drew his attention, even as he threw a second stick of deodorant into his bag. At the rate he was suddenly sweating, he'd need double protection. He glanced into the bedroom and watched Ana explore the area around his bed. For the first time, his mattress looked entirely too big for one person. Two, however, would fit quite nicely.

"It's built into the nightstand," he explained, then grabbed a bottle of aspirin. He'd been fighting a tension headache since his argument with Harper. The agony had just exponentially increased. "Just press the silver button on the end. That connects to the guest room."

The intercom screeched. Before he could disengage the device, Mrs. Bradley's voice asked, "Yes, Mr. St. Cloud?"

"Um, now what do I do?" Ana asked.

"Say goodnight," he grumbled, reaching for the button.

She slapped his hand away. No wonder his sister adored her on sight.

"Goodnight, Mrs. Bradley," she said.

"Oh, Ms. Starling! Were you looking for me? I'm tidying the spare room for Mr. St. Cloud. Do you need anything?"

"No, thank you. But this is a nifty little piece of magic, isn't it?"

Unwilling to listen to his housekeeper and his unexpected guest chat it up over the communication system he'd installed in order to be available to Harper even when he was in his room with the door locked, he snared Ana's wrist and guided her away from the bed.

The minute their flesh made contact, he understood his error. A jolt of heat surged through his system. Her skin was soft as chamois. Her eyes, blue as a spring sky, darkened to charcoal. He snuck a glance down and saw that her nipples were poking pleasurable dents in his cotton jacket.

"Sorry," he said, releasing her. "You've probably been manhandled enough for one night."

"What? Oh, right. Manhandled."

Her voice was throaty and low. For the briefest moment, he wondered if she might not mind being handled by a man with a little more finesse and expertise. A man like him.

"Well, if you need me," he said, moving to leave before he embarrassed himself.

"What will you do?" she asked, grabbing his arm.

Again, a spiral of heat spiked from her fingertips into his bloodstream. Her eyelids were suddenly hooded with what he suspected might be desire.

"If I need you, I mean," she clarified.

He cleared his throat. He wasn't entirely sure if she was coming on to him, but all evidence pointed in that direction. And while he couldn't deny the instant attraction rampaging through his system, he also knew that he'd been abstinent long enough to not trust his instincts. She was a stranger who'd showed up in the bayou in the middle of the night, claiming to be some sort of damsel-in-distress. Wealthy men rarely stayed wealthy when they fell for uninvestigated seductresses who might or might not be as innocent as they appeared.

"I'll alert Mrs. Bradley," he replied. "She's very efficient."

Her lips curved into a tiny frown.

"Good night," he said.

He closed the door behind him and took in a huge breath, trying to blow out the heat that was searing the inside of his lungs. Marching around the corner and toward the stairs, he wasn't entirely surprised to see Harper peeking out of her bedroom at the other end of the hall.

"Well?" she asked.

"You want your punishment for running away now? Geez, Harpy, I thought you'd at least give me until morning to come up with something good."

"You're *so* not punishing me," his sister said, her voice surprisingly confident for a teenager who'd just sneaked out of the house after midnight and returned with someone she'd never set eyes on before. "I meant about Ana. She's pretty, isn't she?"

"I didn't notice," he grumbled.

"Yeah, right. Anyway, I saved her life," Harper continued. "She said she owes me."

"That's ridiculous."

Harper came out of her room and skipped quickly to keep up with his long strides as he turned toward the stairs. "No, it isn't. Stories about life debts are in books, movies, plays. Look at Peter Pettigrew in *Harry Potter.* Azeem and Kevin Costner in *Robin Hood.* Heck, there's even this episode of *The Brady Bunch* where Peter almost gets hit by a falling ladder, but Bobby saves him and—"

"You watch too much television," Jack muttered.

"Only because there isn't much else to do around here."

"You could study," he said, turning on her. "Your French teacher sent me an interesting e-mail about your most recent grade."

"When?"

"Yesterday," he replied.

"You didn't say anything."

"We seemed to have enough to argue about."

He was on the landing when his sister shouted, "Ana speaks French."

"What?"

His sister's clever eyes slashed toward his bedroom. "Ana. She's like a specialist in languages. She could stay here for a while and help me get my grade up. She owes me."

"She has a life," Jack argued, though a quake of anticipation rumbled through his body at the thought of Ana Starling remaining in their household past sunrise. A purely physical response. Because he hadn't had sex in so long.

Again, the image of her standing naked in front of his mirror flashed in his brain. His tongue practically swelled with wanting. Just a taste. A quick, brief sampling. Nothing too filling. Nothing too permanent.

"No, she doesn't," Harper added, bouncing down the stairs. "She told me she was between jobs and that's why she was staying with the friend who has the octopus for a brother. She probably doesn't want to go back after what happened. I bet she'd love to stay. And if she can help me pass French, then her debt to me is repaid."

"You live in a fairytale world, Harper."

She thrust her hands onto her hips. "Only because you won't let me venture into the real one, big brother."

Then her entire demeanor changed. The way she could shift a scene from angry and annoyed to hopeful and giddy in a fraction of a second, Jack knew she had inherited her acting chops from their mother. She slapped her hands together in mock prayer and did that thing with her eyes that somehow made them round and glossy and impossible to ignore.

"Please, Jack. If you won't let me go to Broadway, at least help me pass French. Maybe I'll go on to be a curator at the Louvre. Or study archeology like Belloq in *Indiana Jones*."

At his doubtful stare, she smirked.

"Okay, but it'll be fun to have Ana around for a while. I'm sure she's not a secret serial killer or anything. You can check her out. We haven't had anyone new around here in years."

He tried to keep his face expressionless, but the kid wasn't wrong. Ana was interesting, at the very least.

"I'm bored, Jack," Harper continued, no doubt sensing his weakness. "And so are you. Sooner or later, one of us is going to get into trouble because of it."

Jack knew this was a bad idea, just as he'd known that investing in Nintendo months before they released Wii had been a good one. But Harper was bouncing on the balls of her feet in anticipation and frankly, he hadn't seen her this keen on anything remotely related to school—with the exception of the end-of-the-year musical—in a very long time.

And he wasn't exactly unhappy with the idea of having Ana around, either.

"I'll talk to her about it in the morning," he promised.

Harper leapt up, flung her arms around his neck and kissed his cheek.

"You're the best brother in the universe."

"You didn't think as much a few hours ago."

She danced back up the stairs and turned the corner toward her room, not replying. His sister was smart enough to know when she'd won—which meant Jack now had a tick in the 'lose' column. Making him, officially, a loser. Though judging by his prepubescent reactions to three seconds of his unexpected houseguest's nudity, he certainly couldn't argue.

# 5

ONE REQUIREMENT of fairy godmotherhood was a good night's sleep. At home, down plucked from geese raised on lavender and chamomile had filled her pillows. Her sheets, woven by enchanted silkworms, were cool and fluid in the summer and warm and cozy in the winter. Even her mattress had been stuffed with wool from Bo Peep's infamous flock.

There were *some* perks to servitude.

But while Tatiana guessed that Jack's mattress, sheets and pillows were all top-of-the-line, the fact that they belonged to *him* kept Tatiana wide awake.

She'd done as Jack had suggested and had taken a shower. She'd heard that cold water could douse the internal combustion that came from excessive sexual desire. She'd even prescribed a few icy swims to the occasional over-randy prince. But she learned quickly that a frigid shower was a really stupid idea.

Goosebumps had erupted over her flesh. Her puckered nipples yearned to be enveloped by the heat of Jack's hands and mouth. Icy drops slicing into the curls around her sex drove her to twist the hot-water faucet with such enthusiasm she nearly scalded herself.

And since she'd had no choice but to use his shampoo and soap, sandalwood with subtle hints of amber, cedar and musk clung to her skin as they had to his jacket. He was everywhere and nowhere all at the same time.

Inexplicably hot in the temperature-controlled room, she'd removed the nightshirt Harper had given her. With the lights out and the sheets silky against her skin, Tatiana's every nerve ending itched for attention. And yet, she resisted. She hadn't crossed over between worlds to lose herself in the madness of sexual pleasure. She'd come to grant a wish and gain her freedom.

Though she supposed that if she manipulated the situation well, she could do both.

No. Her personal wishes had to wait. She shoved her hands underneath her pillow and curled into a ball on her side, squeezing her eyes shut. She hadn't known Jack St. Cloud for very long, but her instincts told her that he was an intelligent man who would see through too much subterfuge. She had to focus.

Unfortunately, when she closed her eyes, all she saw was the formidable man marching toward her across his expansive lawn. In her fantasy, however, instead of questioning Tatiana's identity, he pulled her into his arms and kissed her senseless.

Flipping wildly, she punched the pillows a few times, and then tried sleeping flat on her back. Had she been this lusty four centuries ago, before her parents' bargain with the fairies had been revealed?

She squeezed her eyelids tight. Yes. Oh, yes. She'd wanted and lusted and schemed like a woman possessed. The only difference was that then, her youth and inexperience had led her to focus on attaining power rather than sex.

Idiot.

She opened her eyes and turned toward the bedstand. The intercom's tiny silver buttons glittered in the moonlight. One press and she could hear his voice. Maybe she could suggest that he return to his room. Collect something he'd forgotten? Or maybe she could be honest.

*Listen, Jack, I've been celibate and totally unaware of the deliciousness of arousal for four hundred years...want to help me make up for lost time?*

Definitely not a line that would be stolen by poets, that was for sure.

Groaning in frustration, Tatiana grabbed a gold throw

pillow and pitched it at the bedstand, which knocked over a set of decorative candles. A whining noise screamed in the silence and she cursed, figuring that she'd engaged the intercom again. She dove across his bed and punched a few buttons, trying desperately to turn off the device when she heard his voice.

"Ana?"

Sleepy and grouchy and incredibly sexy, Jack's voice rumbled over her, through her, igniting her nerve endings with tiny snaps of fire.

"Yeah," she said. "Sorry. I didn't mean to wake you."

"I wasn't asleep."

Those three words turned her insides to gelatinous goo. She swallowed thickly, wondering if he'd been plagued by the same images and fantasies as she. She had to tread lightly, though. Desire to explore her newfound sexuality was one thing, but what would be the point if she risked her freedom by totally screwing up the situation with Harper?

"Did you need anything?" he asked.

"No, I was just tossing and turning and hit the intercom by accident."

"It's hard to sleep in a strange bed."

She settled into the pillows beneath her, entirely aware of how her nipples had hardened against the cushions simply from hearing his voice. "Sorry I kicked you out of your room."

"That's not what I meant. I didn't mean to imply—"

She laughed. "You didn't. It's okay. I appreciate you taking me in. I want to make it up to you." The evocative suggestion in her whisper was too obvious, so she covered with, "And Harper, too."

But the last bit was lost beneath his question, "Would you like something to help you sleep? A brandy, maybe? I can bring one up."

Was that longing she heard in his voice—a genuine desire to cater to her, perhaps catch another glimpse of her? Because he hadn't fooled her earlier when he'd come into the bedroom. He'd seen her, however briefly, staring at herself in the mirror.

The memory tormented her. Was it tormenting him, as well?

She squeezed her thighs together, trying to dispel the sweet pressure building between her legs at the thought of Jack delivering a brandy to the bedroom only to discover her naked and willing in his bed. This was too much, too soon. Too fast. Too unwise. And Tatiana was anything but unwise.

"Thanks, but I'll be fine," she replied grudgingly.

She had not planned for this turn of events. In her quest to gain her longed-for liberty, she hadn't thought about men or their effect on her new magic-free existence. How could she, when her magical bonds had turned off her ability to experience desire for anything other than freedom?

Even when she'd believed she was on the fast track to being a queen, she'd never thought much about how physical attraction might influence her decision making. She'd flirted and fawned as needed to meet the most available grooms, but she'd never been overwhelmed by such a crushing yearning for anything except a crown.

"Maybe another time?" she suggested.

"Right."

With a groan, Tatiana rolled away from the intercom, pulling a pillow over her head.

Her body was on fire. Her nipples were hard and sensitized so that the sweep of the sheet across them nearly drove her mad. She didn't know much about lust, but she'd witnessed enough hot and heavy interactions between her charges and their lovers to know that if a cold shower didn't do the trick— and it clearly had not—the only way to sate this need was to surrender to it.

Only she couldn't risk a sexual liaison with Jack St. Cloud. She'd have to take care of this herself.

# 6

As Jack rose to pour himself a whiskey, he heard Ana groan and pound a pillow before she disconnected the intercom.

*Yeah, honey. I know how you feel.*

He grabbed a shot of booze and downed it before pouring a more generous serving into a cut-crystal glass and returning to the cold darkness of the guest room. Tempted to bring the whole bottle with him, he remembered that morning wasn't far off. Once the sun rose, he'd either have to get Ms. Ana Starling home—wherever that was—or figure out how to keep her on as Harper's French tutor without losing his sanity. She'd been in his house now for less than two hours and she was doing wicked shit to both his body and his mind.

Just talking to her had him stretched as taut as a regulation pigskin. Hearing her voice so unexpectedly while lying in a bed that was too short for him in a room normally used to store his old football trophies had him wondering just how comfortable she was upstairs on his custom-made mattress. Then he made the mistake of picturing her with her golden hair fanned across his downy pillows, her long, lithe legs peaking out from beneath the comforter—pale and creamy against the silky navy fabric. And then he'd pictured her breasts again. As he downed half of his drink, he heard a noise that slipped into his bloodstream more powerfully than any booze.

A salacious, feminine coo.

He glanced at the intercom. She hadn't turned it off. He opened his mouth to confess that he could still hear her, but another moan broke the silence.

Followed by another.

Then another.

Halfway between whimpers of pleasure and sighs of utter wonder, the sounds coming from Ana Starling's room tackled him like an entire defensive line. If he didn't know she was entirely alone in that room, he'd think she was having sex.

The next, high-pitched gasp convinced him she was—with herself.

He finished his whiskey in one gulp.

A quick check of the intercom controls told him that no other room had access to this erotic soundtrack. He could cut off the connection, but he opted instead to climb back into the tiny queen-size bed, shove a pillow behind his neck and listen.

His eyes drifted closed. The vision of her in front of the mirror materialized with ease. She'd been toying with her nipples, probably watching them extend and harden as blood rushed to her erogenous zone. Was that what she was doing now, drawing her fingernails around her blushing areola, pinching the center nub until sparks of electric need shot through her body, invoking a pounding in her sweet sex?

Jack bit his lip, containing a groan himself as blood rushed from his brain to his groin. His boxers chafed and when he moved to adjust, he couldn't resist holding on to his dick for a good long minute, imagining that she was the one grasping him, stroking him, invoking the madness that was both elemental and cerebral.

A rustle of sheets from her end enflamed the fire consuming him from the inside out. Was she tearing the coverings away to allow herself better access? Her cries grew louder. She seemed unable to catch her breath. He imagined her fingers manipulating her clit with quick little flicks—just like the ones he'd use if he had his tongue on her, in her, around her. His mouth watered. He licked his lips, forcing an explosion of sensation.

How many fingers would it take to bring her to orgasm? How much pressure? What rhythm would push her over the line? Because Jack was finding that a fast and hard pace was working great for him.

Was he thick enough for her? Long enough? Curved enough? His palm was no doubt unequal to the tight, warm wetness he'd discover between her thighs, but it was all he had until he burned off the fire ravaging his body.

The sound of her orgasm was strangled, high-pitched and unrestrained. His was deadly silent. He even grabbed a pillow and pressed it over his mouth to ensure she did not hear a single grunt or groan from him. He moved the cushion just enough to hear her sigh with a satisfaction that echoed like trash talk from a rival team.

So she thought that was an adequate orgasm, did she?

Poor girl had a lot to learn.

Because while he'd soothed one ache in his body, he'd only invoked another. He wanted Ana Starling, but for the life of him, he couldn't figure out how he could possibly have her.

"YOU WANT to go on a what?" he asked his sister when he'd finally forced himself out of bed the next day, sometime before noon. He'd slept like a rock. Wanting to avoid facing Ana so soon after using her masturbatory delight to fuel his own, he'd clung to sleep like a lifeline. It helped that soon after cleaning up all evidence of his handy dispatch of sexual tension, he'd finished off the rest of the whiskey.

Harper poured him a mug of coffee. "A sleepover," Harper said casually, as if she did this every Sunday.

Which she nearly did. Sunday was Mrs. Bradley's day off. The widowed housekeeper usually spent the day with her sister and niece, who lived in the nearby town of Hastings. The niece was Harper's age and attended the same private school in Lunde, another little hamlet twenty minutes away.

Normally, Jack loved these Sundays. With the house empty and the markets closed, he didn't feel so guilty ignoring his work and indulging in his own private pleasures.

But he'd had enough private pleasure last night, thanks.

"What about Ana?" he asked.

"What about her? She's exhausted. She went back to bed."

"You've spoken with her?"

His sister speared him with a look that did not require the accompanying, "Duh."

"I wasn't going to just run off on her, Jack. I do have manners. She said I should spend time with my friends."

"And what are *her* plans?" he asked tentatively.

Harper gave a perfected teenage shrug. "She was barely awake. But I told you, she doesn't feel comfortable going back to her friend's house after last night, so I said it was okay if she hung around for a few days while you worked out the whole tutoring thing."

Jack took a deep breath and pushed down his annoyance with another swallow of scalding coffee. It was his third cup, but he still wasn't feeling the full effects.

"Don't you think you should have consulted with me before you promised a complete stranger safe haven in my home?"

Harper's jaw tensed and her eyes flashed with a look of utter disdain, reminding him of why their mother had indulged the kid so much. Even as a toddler, it had been easier to surrender to Harper rather than battle to the death with her. No one had ever bothered to teach her the meaning of the word *compromise*. Or *capitulation*. He considered himself lucky that she hadn't broached the topic of her Broadway audition again, but he figured she was just biding her time. No matter what he'd said last night, she wouldn't consider the matter closed until she got her way.

Only this time he wasn't giving in. There was too much at stake—more than a fourteen-year-old girl with stars in her eyes could ever understand.

"It's my house, too," Harper said.

"Then you should stick around and entertain your house-guest."

She morphed from incensed to adorable in a flash. "Why? You're the one who needs to check her out and decide if she passes whatever rigorous tests you apply to anyone who wants to get within a half-mile radius of me."

"Not my fault you're worth so much money," he reminded her.

She slid out from the breakfast bar and took her plate with the last remnants of a bagel with strawberry cream cheese to the sink. "I never get to see any of it, so what does it matter if I'm a so-called heiress?"

"When you turn twenty-five, you're going to be stinking rich. It's my job to make sure that no one takes advantage of you before you learn the value of security and financial sense."

"I won't be twenty-five for another eleven years," she whined. "Besides, I don't care about the money. I just want to perform. If I wait until I'm eighteen, I'll be too old and no one in New York will want me."

"Honey, with the portfolio you'll be inheriting, everyone will want you when you're ninety-two and toothless. That's why you have to be so careful. Rich, beautiful, talented— you're a triple threat."

She turned, her expression perplexed. Clearly, she didn't know what to do with his compliment, which made him wonder if he was just a bit too stingy with them.

He took another sip of coffee, then joined her at the sink, placed his hand gently on her shoulder, and tickled her ear in that way she hated.

"Go to your sleepover, Harper. Be a kid. But make sure Ana has everything she needs before you go. I'm going to be working today and I won't have time to entertain her."

Harper launched herself into Jack's arms with such force that he sloshed coffee onto the kitchen floor. But before he could growl at her to help him clean up, she'd shot out of the room. He heard her tennis shoe-shod feet scramble up the stairs and squeak on the hardwood floors as she turned toward his room.

Poor Ana. He hoped she'd slept better than he had, because it was probably going to be a very long, very uncomfortable day.

# 7

CONTRARY TO his expectations, Jack enjoyed a relatively short and relaxing day. Shortly after Mrs. Bradley and Harper had departed, Ana had come downstairs wearing a pretty blue sundress that Harper had ordered for herself over the Internet and neglected to return despite receiving the wrong size. He'd only had a moment to register how amazingly long and lean Ana's legs were before she had announced that she would keep completely out of his hair by spending the day outside.

She'd grabbed a couple of apples and left.

Jack hadn't been able to stop thinking about her all day.

He'd sequestered himself in his studio. Painting had always been his secret passion, something he'd learned to hide from his teammates since high school and from his sister since they'd moved to the bayou. Not because he was ashamed of his work, but because it was his—something he did purely for himself. The *only* thing he did for himself lately.

His current work, as usual, reflected his mood. His brush gravitated toward passionate colors like reds, oranges and purples. And though he'd set out to paint something he could hang in his office, the twists and twirls on the canvas ended up looking suspiciously like a woman's upper torso in the throes of arousal.

Thanks to Ana Starling, he had sex on the brain.

Just after sunset, however, he ventured downstairs to make dinner. Normally Mrs. Bradley left a steak in the fridge for him to toss on the grill.

Tonight, she'd left two.

Just as he was removing the aluminum foil, Ana wandered inside. Her hair was windblown and a little frizzy. Her face glowed with sweat.

"You've been gone a long time," he said, surprised when the words came out more as an accusation than an observation.

She didn't seem to notice. "You have beautiful property here. So much to do and see."

He eyed her suspiciously. The bayou, to him, was indeed striking, overflowing with tall, mossy trees, still waters and so many different plants and animals a botanist or zoologist could study an entire lifetime and never catalogue them all. However, in his experience, most women found the place primitive and creepy. Jane, the girl he might have married before his mother had died, had spent two weeks in what she called "the swamp" and departed without a backward glance.

"You really think so?"

She looked at him as though he'd sprung a second head. "I don't say things I don't mean."

"Duly noted," he said with a nod. "So, while I've got you in an honest mood, do you like steak or are you some kind of vegan tree-hugger?"

She winced. "Hug trees? Where I'm from, trees are very grabby."

He chuckled, but he wasn't entirely certain she was joking.

"And where *are* you from?"

"Far from here," she replied.

"Can you be a little more specific?"

Her eyes darted to the side before she replied, "England."

"Really?" he asked, not believing her for a minute, even if he realized now that she did sport something of an accent. "Whereabouts?"

"London."

Easy enough to check out.

He rinsed the aluminum foil in the sink and threw it into the recycle bin. "So, you're a carnivore, then?"

She looked at him, clearly perplexed. He lifted a steak on the tine of a long fork.

"Oh, yes. Do you cook?"

"In the bayou, all men cook. Why don't you pick out a nice bottle of wine while I get a marinade going?"

He pointed to the wine cooler. He didn't drink a lot, but clients sent him expensive vintages all the time. Notwithstanding his revelry last night with the only other Jack in this house—Jack Daniels—he rarely drank alone. Ana returned moments later with a bottle he never would have picked. The label was bright blue and featured a fairy surrounded by elves. It was a Gewürztraminer called Kissed.

He was suddenly very, very thirsty.

"You know this one?" he said, tilting the bottle back toward her.

Ana scanned the label carefully, her eyes wide with innocence.

"Hmm, I've never seen her before, but I do like her fashion sense."

More than once during the leisurely preparation of dinner, Jack had reason to believe that he and Ana were speaking the same language, but with entirely different meaning. As he rubbed the steaks with garlic and olive oil and directed her in the proper way to stir polenta until it was creamy and smooth, they chatted about everything and nothing. She was entirely noncommittal on topics like politics and religion and seemed ignorant of sports and pop culture outside of Disney movies and fantasy literature. She did like talking about art, so by the time he pulled the ribeyes off the grill and served them up with a crisp salad, polenta seasoned with smoky mushrooms and a second bottle of wine, it was nearly eight o'clock and he had the sinking suspicion that he now knew her very well, even though he hardly knew her at all.

"So, about this tutoring thing," he said, finally ready to broach the subject. He refilled her wineglass, this time with a red that he'd chosen—one that wasn't named anything suggestive.

"You seem reluctant," she said instantly, taking a bite of the creamy Italian grits and showing her appreciation by closing her eyes and moaning.

He dropped his fork.

Her eyes flashed open. "You okay?"

Another swallow of wine calmed his rapidly beating heart. The sound was familiar—too familiar. He may not know Ana's opinions on the current economic status of the banking industry, but he knew her more intimately than he would ever admit. You didn't listen to a woman pleasure herself without learning a few things.

Things that could be useful.

If the circumstances were different.

Which they weren't.

"I'm fine," he said. "I'm glad you're enjoying your meal."

"I like a man who knows his way around a kitchen," she said. "I never learned to cook, but working with you was fun. You made it fun."

The warmth spawned by the cabernet sauvignon spread lower than his stomach. He couldn't deny it anymore—Ana Starling was beautiful, funny and knew how to deliver a compliment in a way that made him believe she was entirely sincere. How long had it been since a woman had come into his life, however accidentally, and made him feel not like a repressive big brother or a skillful investment broker, but just a man?

An attractive man. A fun guy. One worth listening to. One, perhaps, worth kissing?

Her choice of wine earlier could not have been an accident. Of course, her audioerotic performance last night might have been on purpose, too. But if she'd come to the bayou specifically to seduce him, why had she spent the entire day staying out of his way?

So many questions.

"How do you know French?" he asked.

"Studied it my entire life," she replied. "Well, since I was seventeen. One of my job requirements."

"You were a teacher?"

She grinned, her eyes twinkling, as if she possessed some sort of secret she wasn't yet willing to share. "I've worked with a lot of young people, imparting my knowledge in very effective ways."

He leaned his elbow on the table and cradled his chin on his palm. "How would you approach helping Harper?"

She chewed her mouthful of salad, took another sip of wine and thought about her answer. "I think I'd start with focusing on words that have meanings that apply to her life. Words about music and theater and—"

"No," he declared. "She gets enough of that."

"Why do you hate the arts so much?"

"I don't hate the arts. I appreciate music and theater more than most. How could I not, considering my parents' careers?"

"I know about your mother from Harper, but she didn't mention that your father was in the entertainment industry."

"He was a producer. A money man, like me. And one of his favorite investments was art. He collected Monet, Degas, Van Gogh. Even a Renoir or two. He sat on the board of several museums."

She nodded, but not as if she actually understood the magnitude of what he'd said. Bartholomew St. Cloud hadn't exactly been a man's man. He'd been suave and sophisticated, tall and broad, but completely unimpressed by athletics unless it was tennis, squash or polo.

Jack, now that he was older, guessed that his own initial interest in football had been a means of rebellion. Funny how things worked out, though. Because as soon as Bart had witnessed his eight-year-old son's first peewee league game, the sophisticated man had become the biggest fan of the sport Jack had ever seen.

He'd even been buried with Jack's college jersey.

The memory demanded another sip of wine.

"And your mother was an actress," Ana supplied, seeming to sense his sudden discomfort.

"A famous one," he volunteered. "I can't believe you've never heard of her."

"Who says I haven't? As I recall, she played in the West End version of *Once Upon a Mattress,* am I right?"

Her eyes, which he noticed were a particularly dark and mesmerizing shade of sapphire blue, brightened. She slid another forkful of polenta into her mouth, letting her lashes flutter down against her cheeks while she expressed, yet again, her flavorful delight.

Full of surprises, this one. She knew more than she let on—dropping information like penalty flags. If only he hadn't been alone for so long, he might have gathered the strength to block her allure. But he was a man who'd been without any available, beautiful women for quite a long time.

And he couldn't resist her—not even if he tried.

Resisting, however, was suddenly the last thing on his mind.

# 8

THE WINE was making her woozy.

This was a surprising development, since in her world, wine was the drink of choice. Fermented grape juice flowed from jugs at every dinner, ball or party she'd ever attended and she'd never once felt as if thin layers of skin were the only thing keeping her insides contained. The feeling made it hard for her to stand beside Jack as they cleared off dishes and placed them in a remarkable invention called a dishwasher. Like a kitchen maid, but without the back talk.

"It's late. Ready for bed?" Jack asked as he shut the door to the marvelous appliance.

She turned and rested back on her hands, which gripped the edge of the sink.

"Am I ever," she replied, sounding breathless, which was appropriate, since her lungs suddenly weren't working as effortlessly as usual.

"I guess that sounded like a come-on," he commented, one eyebrow tilting upward.

He had gorgeous brown eyes. Dark and rich and expressive. She leaned forward, interested to see how his pupils reacted when she neared.

"Did it?" she asked.

The brown irises darkened to almost black. She might not be experienced with men on a personal level, but she was a quick study.

According to the plan dictated to her this morning before

Harper left for her sleepover, Tatiana was supposed to spend the day buttering Jack up so he would agree to Harper's audition in New York—or at the very least, to securing her position as a French tutor so she'd have more time to convince him that Harper possessed a rare talent that shouldn't be locked away. But once Tatiana had fully awakened, she'd decided on a different tack.

First, she'd given him space, to prove she wouldn't be a distraction to his comfortable, ordered life. She'd spent the entire day outdoors, exploring the landscape, napping in a hammock and trying not to replay the erotic dreams that had haunted her all night—the ones where Jack's hands, rather than her own, were pleasuring her body.

So far, her plan seemed to be working nicely. Since she'd reentered the house, he'd given her his undivided attention. He'd wanted to know everything about her. She realized he was testing to see if she was worthy of contact with his sister, but she also hoped that some of his questions were personal.

"Do you often flirt with men you barely know?" he asked.

She shook her head. "I never do."

He lifted the other eyebrow. "Never?"

"Never," she repeated, meeting his gaze straight on.

"So why now?"

She wasn't certain he was aware of it, but he'd invaded her personal space deeply enough for her to finally identify the mystery scent mingling with dizzying amber and heady musk.

"Do you paint?"

He retreated just as unconsciously as he'd advanced. She snagged him by his shirt, tugged him forward and buried her nose in the fabric.

"That's definitely paint. Oils." She peered upward, but did not release him. "You're a man with secrets."

"Everyone has secrets," he whispered, his breath teasing the wisps of hair on her forehead.

"True, but I don't think it's any big secret that I'm attracted to you. And unless I'm reading the signs wrong," she said, fully aware of how her belly brushed against his erection, "you want me, too."

He wrapped his hands around hers and disengaged her fingers from his shirt. She had no idea she'd been holding him so tightly until she saw the wrinkled fabric.

"As I've told my sister many times, we can't always get what we want."

"Why not?"

"Because what we want may not be the best thing for us."

"That's a reasonable argument," she said, recognizing that Jack St. Cloud was a man whose mind demanded just as much exercise as his body. "But what could be wrong about us?"

He opened his mouth to answer, but she held up her hand.

"Nothing beyond tonight," she said. "I totally get you need to be a role model for your sister and that you have to look out for her best interests above all else, which is why I want to tutor her and help show you how bright and determined she is. But she's not here now, Jack. It's just you and me. I've never felt an attraction this powerful before."

"You use that word a lot," Jack said.

"What word?"

"Never."

"Up until I came to your bayou, my life was pretty simple. Filled with absolutes." She moved closer to him with each word, finally splaying her hands over his chest as if to smooth out the crinkles she'd put in his shirt, but in reality, to caress the rock-hard muscles underneath. "For instance, I've *never* had a man excite me so much. And with only one exception, I've always gotten everything I want."

"What's the one exception?"

"Can't say," she replied, snaking her fingers up to his collar, then to his chin where she swiped her thumbs across his lips. His mouth was suddenly very moist and very appealing.

Just the thought of kissing him made her waver.

Luckily, he grabbed her by the elbows and held her steady.

"Why can't you tell me?" he whispered, lowering his head one inch, then one more.

"You'd never believe me."

"You could convince me," he murmured.

"I intend to—"

But her objective was cut off mid-sentence when his lips pressed so tentatively against hers, she wondered if the kiss was real or just an alcohol-induced dream. She forced her eyes open just as he spread his hands on her waist and tugged her closer. Suddenly, he wasn't playing games. His tongue slipped into her mouth and did such delicious things with hers that she couldn't help moaning in sheer appreciation.

His shoulders were broad and steady under her exploring fingers. His neck tightened with what she imagined to be restraint, though his lips were giving no quarter. The swirl of his tongue, the nip of his teeth, the skillful way he turned his head so he could deepen the kiss nearly caused her to forget to breathe. When he pulled away, she stumbled a little.

"Wow," she said.

A corner of his lips quirked upward. "Like that, huh?"

"Do you always ask questions where the answer is obvious?"

"I haven't asked you enough questions," he countered, self-reproach in his tone.

She narrowed her eyes, grabbed his shirt again and lifted herself so they were as close to eye-to-eye as she could get with a man who was a good eight inches taller than she was. "I haven't told you everything about myself yet, but I swear that there is nothing in my past, present or future that could hurt you or your sister. Can you say the same?"

"Definitely."

"Then shut up and kiss me."

He took direction very, very well. In an instant, he'd swept her into his arms and carried her up the stairs, kissing her wildly even as he kicked open the door to his bedroom. She might have lost her wings when she crossed the barrier between her world and his, but she was flying nonetheless.

The door rebounded off the wall and shut with a thud just as he laid her on the bed and held his body over hers. Touching, but not touching—except for his lips.

She worked the buttons of his shirt, her fingers shaking with anticipation. He untied the straps on her dress and, after she yanked his shirt off, he lowered his head and took her nipple into his mouth so that an explosion of sensation rocked her to her core.

"Oh!" she exclaimed.

He chuckled against her skin and the vibration sent another flutter of delight scurrying across her flesh. He cupped her breasts with his hands and laved the sensitive skin until she was tossing her head back and forth against the pillows, denying the flood of ecstasy that threatened to drown her. She'd touched herself last night, yes. But she'd experienced nothing like this.

"You're so sensitive," he said, flicking his stiff tongue across her nipple.

"I can hardly—"

He took her fully into his mouth and sucked hard, using his hand to attend to the other breast while he created spirals of electricity with his tongue.

"Jack, don't—" she said.

He looked up, his dark eyes befuddled.

"I'll come," she explained.

His confusion turned to pure, wicked intent.

"That's the idea."

He switched to the other breast. His fingers plucked as his mouth pulled. She jammed her hands into his hair, unable to resist the pleasure flooding through her body. And yet, it wasn't enough. She needed more. So much more. She rocked her pelvis upward to press against the hardness in his groin.

Then, before she could think, his hands were beneath her hem. Past her panties. He parted the flesh at the juncture of her thighs and he inserted a finger into her moist passage. She nearly bucked off the bed, soaring again. Before she landed,

*Into the Woods*

he drove a second finger inside her. Then a third, curving the tips to touch her so that she rocketed even higher.

"Jack," she begged. "Please. Stop. I'll—"

"Come on, sweetheart. Take it. Enjoy it. Let me watch you come before I've even taken off my clothes."

She had no strength and no desire to deny him. She spread her legs and in seconds, she was flying above her body. A sizzling cloud of ecstasy blinded her to anything except the swirls of sensation coursing around her, through her, within her.

When the spasms started to subside, so did the intensity of his kiss until a tiny brush of his lips over her nose left her utterly breathless.

# 9

JACK COULD NOT tear his gaze from Ana's, mesmerized by the way her pupils had expanded until he was certain he'd blinded her with pleasure. Although he'd made love with many women, particularly in his younger days, he'd never watched a lover orgasm without taking some of the gratification for himself. But after hearing her come last night, he'd had to see for himself if she was as captivating in ecstasy as he'd imagined.

She was.

And then some.

He took care to smooth her skirt down, but could not find the power to cover her spectacular breasts. Her nipples weren't quite as taut as they had been at the height of pleasure, but they were puckered and red and a little raw. His mouth watered for another taste, but instead of giving in to temptation, he pushed off the bed, shrugged out of the rest of his clothes, and then dashed into the bathroom to retrieve the condoms.

When he returned, he found her curled toward him, her eyes wide and hungry as her gaze swept down his naked body. When she spied his erection, she licked her lips.

"Thank you," she said, her tone shy but her stare brazen.

He chuckled. "My pleasure, believe me."

She shook her head, her expression almost serious as he slid onto the bed beside her. "What do you like?" she asked.

Lovers had asked him that question before, but never without the sly, seductive lilt of a woman who knew precisely how to do whatever wild thing he requested. Ana's voice hinted at an innocent and yet innate curiosity that suddenly made him wonder just how much she knew about men. Or about lovemaking.

"I'm a guy. We pretty much like everything."

She laughed. "Yeah, that much I gathered. But, if I were, to say, touch you like this," she said, softly sweeping her hand over his erection, "would that be enough?"

"No," he answered.

She ringed her fingers around him, squeezing tightly. "How about this?"

He swallowed thickly. "Better."

She drew the circle of pressure upward, stopping only when her grip met the ridge of his head. "Is this too slow?"

This time, he could only nod.

She slid her hand down to the base of his dick and then pulled up hard. He winced.

"Okay," she said. "I've got it now."

And boy, did she. Ten seconds later and he was lost in the hand job of all hand jobs. She found a rhythm almost instantly, one that pushed him to the brink with sheer precision. And she wasn't quiet about her excitement at witnessing how his cock got longer and thicker. She practically squealed with delight when a drop of semen oozed from the tiny hole at the tip.

"Looks so pearly and creamy," she said.

"Taste it," he urged, too wild with lust to couch his words.

"Don't mind if I—"

She kissed her way down his chest and when she flicked her tongue across him, he nearly came undone. He grabbed the dark sheets, scrunching them in his fists, willing his body to hang on and not surrender too soon. She kissed along the thick ridges of his sex, cupping his balls and squeezing tighter in her enthusiasm.

"Suck me," he asked.

"Really?"

It was as if he'd awarded her some spectacular trophy, until she wrapped those wonderful lips completely around him. Then, he was the one who'd won the award of a lifetime. He had a Heismann of a hard-on and she was loving every inch of it, alternating between using friction and suction and moans of delight to make him wonder if he'd died and gone to heaven. Her hands, her teeth and her tongue drove him so close to the edge that he found himself tangling his fingers into her hair and pulling her off only seconds before he exploded.

He intended to come more than once tonight, but each and every time, he wanted to be buried deep inside her.

He had the condom on in record time. He'd always been known for his speed on the field, but by the time he had her back underneath him, his erection pressed at the entrance to her sweet sex, he'd made the decision to take it slowly. Maybe it was the wonder in her eyes. Maybe it was the way she worried her bottom lips with her teeth. Maybe it was the insatiable need to make this last for as long as he possibly could.

"Now what do I do?" she asked.

The question caught him off guard. His chest tightened and he attempted to pull back, but she stopped him.

"You've never—"

"No," she replied.

"Then I can't," he started, but her watering eyes stopped him cold. He hadn't knowingly bedded a virgin since he'd been one himself. He couldn't imagine what circumstances had led a woman as sensual and beautiful as Ana to save herself this long, but he doubted that having sex with a virtual stranger her first time was something she'd be happy about in the morning.

However, she grabbed him by the upper arms and dug her nails in deep. "Don't stop."

"You'll regret this," he said.

"Believe me, Jack, of all the things I'll regret in my life, this will not be one."

She reached down between them and though she gasped at the slippery feel of the condom, she guided him toward her hot entrance, then grabbed his buttocks and pulled him to the edge of ecstasy.

He swallowed thickly, trying—and failing—to resist.

"Jack, feel how wet I am. How tight. I've waited so long. Don't make me wait another…"

He didn't. Exercising more control than he knew he possessed, he pressed inside her in infinitesimal increments. She spread her legs wide, gasping softly as her snug flesh opened for him. When her fingernails burrowed into his skin, he stopped.

"Am I hurting you?" he asked.

"Only when you stop," she replied.

"Give me your hands."

She complied. He threaded his fingers with hers and held them high above her head.

"Now, wrap your legs around my waist. Higher. Yeah, right there."

He'd slid entirely inside her and the sensation made them both groan. He paused, reveling in the feel of her taut wetness enveloping him, but then she started to writhe, lighting the fuse. He withdrew, then pressed deeper, sliding toward complete release.

"Oh, Jack!" she said, turning her face to the side, her expression wide-eyed, as if the sensations surprised her.

"How do I feel?"

"Wonderful, I can't…" she said, losing the battle for words in her war to breathe.

"You're so hot," he confessed, driving deep and then pulling back, forcing himself to milk every possible sensation from her body into his.

She tightened her legs around his waist and moved in a counter rhythm that enhanced the sensations one hundred times.

"Ana, don't. Ana, stop. Ana. Don't. Stop."

He kissed her just before he came and in the middle of the mind-numbing experience, he realized she hadn't fully joined him for the ride. She was still rocking beneath him, desperate for the release he'd just enjoyed. He let go of one of her hands and slipped his fingers between them, toggling her clit until she screamed in rapture and her spasms matched his throb for throb.

When the waves of pleasure subsided, he kissed her again, got up from the bed and disposed of the condom. Then, remembering her inexperience, he grabbed a soft cloth from the drawer under his sink, doused it with warm water and returned to the bed.

She hadn't moved. She was staring at the ceiling, still attempting to regulate her breathing. He slid onto the bed beside her and pressed the moist towel to her sex.

"Ooh," she moaned. "That feels amazing."

"You're amazing. You're sure this was your first time?"

She laughed. "I'm fairly positive."

"How was I?"

She turned her face and those dark blue eyes sparkled with wickedness. "Hmm. If I say there's room for improvement, will you be too insulted to try again? And if I say you were perfect, then why attempt to improve?"

"So I'm gathering you want to do this again?"

"Yes, Jack. I do. And the sooner, the better."

# 10

SINCE LOSING her powers, Tatiana had accepted her inability to fly, but she suspected that by morning, walking was going to be a challenge, as well. But she'd never felt so full, so satisfied, so sore and so beautiful in her entire existence.

So this was what it felt like to be a woman—a real, flesh-and-blood human woman whose power came not from spells or wands, but from the exploration and release of her sexuality. After mating with a man who'd made her feel cherished when he barely knew her, she'd been tempted more than once to cry.

Dawn approached. Jack had wrapped her in an oversized terrycloth robe and led her onto the balcony outside his bedroom. He'd brought coffee, which he'd sweetened with milk and sugar, then cuddled with her on an outdoor chaise lounge. While she watched the sun streak slashes of pink and lavender into the morning sky, he watched her.

"You are incredibly beautiful," he said.

If the morning light wasn't so uncertain, she was sure he'd have seen her blush.

"Why haven't you made love with anyone before now?" he asked.

"Is knowing important to you?"

"It shouldn't be, but it is."

She couldn't lie to him. Not after what they'd shared.

"I never wanted to make love before. But the minute I saw you walk across the lawn, I wanted you for myself. Even if only for one night."

The situation forced her to give him that out clause—to

ensure that he didn't whisk her away before she'd had a chance to fulfill Harper's wishes. As much as she wanted to relive the sensation of accepting his body into hers again, with the rising sun came the hard truth that she didn't have forever to convince Jack to allow Harper to sing for the Broadway producers—and consequently, free her from her bonds.

She had less than a month—from the waning full moon to the rising. And though they'd gone an entire evening without discussing his sister's situation, she was certain that having sex with Jack would not change his mind about Harper. The man who'd made love to her all night long was not the same man who had built such constricting parameters around Harper's life.

"Do you want this to be a one-night deal?" he asked.

"No," she replied, again putting her faith in the truth.

"I don't want this to be one night, either," he confessed, curling his fingers in the strands of her hair. "But I can't risk Harper finding out about us. She's only fourteen. I'm supposed to be her role model and she looks up to you, too. I'm not great at this parenting thing, but explaining casual sex to the one person I never want to *have* casual sex is…problematic."

Tatiana understood. This world was wholly unlike Elatyria, but cherishing a young girl's chastity was pretty universal on both sides of the bayou.

"Do you want me to leave?"

"What? No!" He'd sat up and she watched conflict skitter across his expression just like the birds rising off the wetlands in the distance. "I don't want you to go."

She attempted to cover a satisfied smile. "Aren't I complicating your life?"

"Maybe my life hasn't been complicated enough lately."

"I don't think Harper would agree with you."

"Maybe that's the problem. Maybe I'm so focused on her and have been for so long, I've forgotten to take some things for myself."

He relaxed against her and they remained there, dozing when

they weren't chatting, occasionally touching and kissing, until the passion stoked hot again and Jack carried her back inside, closed the patio doors and drew the curtains so it was almost like night again. They made love one more time in such slow motion, Tatiana attempted to memorize each moment as it happened. She replayed each and every sensation before the next delight occurred. From his lips on her neck to his tongue on her breasts to his sex sliding oh-so-gently into hers.

They were seconds from climaxing when the intercom beside Jack's bed buzzed.

He rolled her atop him as he reached for the button on the bedstand. She had to use all of her self-control to keep quiet at the new explosion of sensations. His sex speared her most sensitive spot, knocking every single thought from her mind except the edict to remain quiet.

"Yes, Mrs. Bradley?"

"I just wanted to let you know I've returned. Harper got off to school just fine. I have a few loads of laundry to do and then I'm off to the market."

"I'm in desperate need of—" he started, plucking at Tatiana's breasts so that she threw her head back and bit her lip trying to keep from screaming with pleasure. "…shaving cream. Can you head…to the market first?"

"You had three cans in your bath last time I checked," Mrs. Bradley argued.

Tatiana slid her hands into the hair on Jack's chest and tugged hard, adjusting her knees so that suddenly, she ruled the timing and intensity of their lovemaking. She moved her hips, lifting up high and then inching back down on him. Every single nerve ending inside her caught fire—and clearly, the same sensation burned through Jack, as well.

"I…must…have…" Jack said, breathing hard, bracing his hands on her waist in a valiant but useless attempt to keep her still. "…used it all up. Get some more, will you?"

"And what about Ms. Starling?"

Jack groaned, but the sound was so low and restrained,

Tatiana was certain that only she had heard. "She's…just… fine. Please, Mrs. Bradley. I'm quite busy and I need that shaving—"

He clicked off the intercom just in time. Neither could hold back their orgasms any longer. They pumped hard and cried out together. Tatiana fell against his heaving chest, utterly spent and completely and totally enamored.

Which wasn't good. But she couldn't find the energy to care. She had a month to convince him about Harper. Couldn't she enjoy Jack as a lover rather than an adversary just a little while longer?

JACK COULDN'T REMEMBER the last time Harper had been angry with anyone other than himself. Yet, as he watched his sister's stare bore into Ana from across the dinner table, he was certain that if looks could kill, his new lover would be on her way to the morgue.

"You're being rude," he announced.

Ana looked up at both of them. Concentrating on reviewing Harper's homework as they ate, she hadn't noticed his sister's murderous gaze.

"I'm sorry," Ana said, apparently thinking his censure was meant for her. "But I wanted to make sure that—"

"Not you," Jack replied. "Harper. She hasn't said a word to you since we sat down and you haven't noticed because you've been helping her with her homework instead of enjoying your meal so she doesn't have to miss her favorite television show."

Harper trained her hate-filled stare at him. "It's not my fault I had to do detention after school." Her words trailed a bit at the end when she realized how ridiculous her claim sounded.

And still, Jack couldn't resist.

"Oh, then precisely whose fault was it? Because last time I checked, the school was clear on the fact that writing mathematical formulas on the bottom of your shoe so you could sneak a peek at them during a test was not acceptable behavior."

Harper pushed her plate away. "I'm not hungry. May I be excused?"

Ana looked between them, utter confusion on her face.

The honeymoon period was over.

For two weeks following Ana's unexpected insertion into their household, the three of them had existed in pure bliss. During the days while Harper was at school, Jack spent the mornings conducting business and the afternoons making love to his sister's live-in tutor. Once Harper came home, Ana turned her attention completely on his sister—not only helping her with French, but checking over her history and literature studies and learning about the wonders of Google. In the evenings, the three of them enjoyed the type of rare, family-style dinners that Jack had seen only on sitcoms. Mrs. Bradley also joined them on occasion, electing to share her delicious cooking with the trio even though the older woman usually preferred to eat in her room with the television tuned to her prerecorded soap operas.

Best of all, Harper had not mentioned the Broadway audition once. And her grades, after only fourteen days, had started to hit the A range with surprising regularity.

In fact, everything had improved. Jack found himself not only smiling a lot more often, but whistling, too. Even his workouts resulted in higher endorphins and the attendant euphoria. Since he'd retired from the gridiron, he'd lifted weights and jogged through the bayou to burn off tension. Now, he was exercising to keep in shape and improve his flexibility.

And until tonight, there had been very little tension left to burn off.

"What's your problem, Harper?" he asked, at the same time that Ana said, "Did something happen at school today?"

Harper skewered him first. "My problem is you." Then, she turned to Ana. "And no, nothing happened at school. Nothing ever happens at school. Nothing ever happens in my whole life. It's day after day of nothing. Oh, just forget it!"

She pushed away from the table, grabbed her plate and threw it into the sink with such force that Jack was sure it had shattered—he couldn't see for sure since they'd taken to eating in the dining room rather than at the kitchen island.

He moved to stand, but Ana laid her hand on his arm.

"I don't think this is about you," she said gently, leaning forward and kissing him, injecting him with that special brand of calm that only she provided. "Let me talk to her."

She stood, giving him a chance to take her hand and sweep a kiss across her knuckles. "You don't have to."

"Yeah," she said with a wink. "I think I do."

She sauntered out of the room and since they were alone, gave her hips a little extra swing, making his entire body taut with need. She might have been new to lovemaking two weeks ago, but she'd caught on like a pro. Fearless and curious, Ana had inspired Jack to a whole new perspective on sex. Heck, she'd forced him to consider a whole new perspective on his life.

He rose to clear the rest of the table, but his cell phone rang. Noting the caller on the LCD screen, he cursed, left the dishes and instead went into the study, shutting the door behind him.

# *11*

"HEY, SEAN," Jack greeted his caller. "What have you got for me?"

"No more than I had last week," the private investigator replied. "If there's an Ana Starling who has ever been in any trouble in the United States, she's not the one living in your house."

Jack slipped into the leather chair behind his desk and kicked his heels up. He'd called his friend, Sean Devlin, whom he'd met through his lawyer, to investigate Ana the day after they'd made love the first time. Guilt had niggled at him ever since, but while Harper was heiress to the vast St. Cloud fortune, he was worth even more. Since his forced retirement from the NFL, he'd parlayed his signing bonuses and first two years' salary and endorsements into a massive portfolio. Although Ana struck him as extremely honest, he was pretty sure she was hiding something.

Unfortunately, Sean had yet to dig up what it was.

"Any avenues left for you to explore?" Jack asked.

Sean clucked his tongue. "Man, I've done all the regular searches and then some. Unless she's some sort of international spy with covert protections, she's just a chick who happened on your isolated doorstep. From the picture you sent me from your cell phone, she's smoking hot. You know what they say about gift horses, right?"

Jack chuckled. "Can't be too careful."

"This is true," Sean replied. "But you've been the most careful dude I've known since you moved back to Louisiana.

Wasn't caution that got you onto the Giants' roster, man. Or that built those bank accounts that allow you to pay me the big bucks. You should go for it."

"I thought PIs were supposed to be jaded when it came to relationships."

"I didn't say shit about a relationship," Sean clarified. "I just meant that she's probably safe to nail."

"I never realized you were such a dog," Jack said.

"You could pay me in Milk-bones, brother, but I'll settle for cash," the investigator cracked with an unrepentant snicker before disconnecting the call.

Well, there it was. He'd had Ana checked out as thoroughly as possible. Last week Sean had found a woman named Anna Sterling who held a British passport, but misspellings aside, he'd been unable to confirm that the woman in the picture Jack had sent him and the woman whose grainy photo was in the international database was the same person. No one named Ana Starling possessed a criminal record.

And yet, ever since Harper had returned from a pre-arranged two-hour detention on account of her attempt to cheat on her math test, his sister had been treating Ana like Public Enemy Number One.

Why? And if Ana couldn't get to the root of the problem, where would it leave them?

"I DON'T WANT to talk to you," Harper said, swiping at the tears that had been streaming, unbidden, down her face before Tatiana had had the nerve to follow her to her room.

"Then you can listen," Ana retorted, placing the homework she'd been checking on Harper's desk and then sliding onto the foot of her bed.

Harper grabbed the remote control to her flat screen, aimed it at the television and turned the volume up as loud as it went. She wasn't even sure what program was on. She didn't even care. She just wanted to shut out the reprimands she was certain she was about to hear from a woman she'd expected to take her side. And yet, when Jack had grounded her over the math test, Tatiana hadn't even said a word in Harper's defense!

Tatiana arched an eyebrow and then, in a move that was quicker than Harper would ever have imagined, swiped the remote out of her hand and turned the television off.

"What do you think you're doing?"

"Talking to you," she insisted, though calmly, which infuriated Harper even more.

"Just exactly who do you think you are? Coming into my room uninvited. Waltzing around my brother's house as if you own the place. Making me *really* study French! This wasn't what our deal was supposed to be about!"

She grabbed the crown-shaped pillow Jack had given her last Christmas and hugged it to her chest. She hated sounding like such a child, but she was completely pissed off. The woman had been in her house for an entire two weeks and she hadn't yet convinced her brother to let her go to New York to audition. In fact, she was pretty certain Tatiana hadn't even brought up the subject yet, much less persuaded him to change his mind.

"I understand," Tatiana said.

"No, you don't," she countered. "You have everything you want! You're living in this great house with this ready-made family. Only we're not your family. I'm just some girl who found you in the woods and who somehow believed your whacked-out story about being lost and wanting to help me and my brother is just a guy who can't take his eyes off your rack."

The words were supposed to hurt and yet, Tatiana gave the tank top she'd purchased during a shopping trip with Mrs. Bradley a defiant tug.

"I *am* trying to help you," she insisted. "Apparently you haven't noticed, but your brother has been awfully nice to be around lately, hasn't he? Easy to laugh. Relaxed. Not trying to schedule every minute of your day. If you hadn't pulled that stupid trick in your math class, I might have been able to talk to him about your audition tonight."

Harper opened her mouth to argue, but no matter how

furious she was, she couldn't deny the truth. Jack *had* been laughing a lot lately. He'd even come up to her room a few nights ago and watched TV with her. He'd loosened the reins on her study schedule since Tatiana had taken over supervising her schoolwork, trusting when Tatiana decided that Harper had done enough. She'd actually had time to go into her studio to rehearse without feeling as though Jack was going to bust in any minute and yell at her to forget about music and study, study, study!

Of course, it was because she'd been working on a new song that she'd ignored her upcoming algebra test, which had resulted in her spontaneous decision to scribble the formulas on the bottom of her shoe. She'd convinced herself that she'd get away with the old-school trick since teachers nowadays only confiscated cell phones and backpacks to keep kids from cheating.

Unfortunately, her math teacher was old-school enough to catch her glancing at her sole one time too many.

"Well, I did my detention and I took the zero on the test. So now when are you going to talk to Jack about the audition?" Harper asked, pushing aside the sinking suspicion that yet again, she'd been her own worst enemy.

Tatiana scooted closer and plucked at the silver sequins that spelled out the word, *Princess* on her pillow. "I was going to ask him tonight."

"So do it," Harper encouraged.

"After you just proved yourself wholly incapable of making the right moral choice? Harper, honey, I've been using your computer during the day to research this Broadway. It's in New York City. I've heard about that place. I once knew this prin—um, girl," she said, stumbling over a word, "whose stepmother arranged for her to go there. She had no idea what she was doing and could have gotten into a whole lot of trouble except she was lucky enough to find this guy who—"

Harper rolled her eyes. "If you're trying to scare me with some story of a friend's self-destruction in the big, bad city, you're preaching to the choir. I know what happened to my mom there. She got mixed up with the wrong crowd and drank a lot and ignored her responsibilities and contracts. I'm not going to do any of that. I just want to sing!"

Tatiana frowned. "How is Jack supposed to believe you when you can't make the right choice about an algebra test?"

Harper cursed and threw the pillow across the room, knocking over a collection of perfume bottles she'd inherited from her mother—the kind with the little squeeze balls at the end of tubes, that singers used to fill with special tonics to soothe their throats.

"He can hire anyone he wants to look after me! You can do it," she offered. "It would be great. You could come with me and tutor me in all my classes. If I nail this audition, I'm sure the producers would pay for you to teach me. Jack knows you and likes you. It's perfect!"

Tatiana shifted backward, her teeth tugging on her bottom lip. Her sudden reluctance hit Harper hard.

"You don't want me to go, either."

"I didn't say that," Tatiana shot back, though it wasn't quite the denial Harper wanted to hear. "But if you want me to fulfill your wish to go to New York City with Jack's approval, then you're going to have to prove to him that you're a responsible young woman who won't be tempted to do the wrong thing just because it's easier."

"He would have freaked out if I'd failed that math test," she argued.

"And he's not freaking out now that you cheated?" Tatiana countered.

Harper huffed and tried to keep her tears at bay, but one stupid drop escaped from each of her eyes and trickled down her cheeks. "Okay, okay! I screwed up. I made a stupid choice and I got caught. What do I do now?"

Finally, Tatiana's familiar and pretty smile returned. Harper really could see why Jack seemed so happy lately. He was, after all, a man—even if the idea of her brother being romantically involved with anyone made her stomach hurt. She supposed he had to be lonely living out in the bayou without anyone around except for Mrs. Bradley and her.

Tatiana patted Harper's thigh, then rose to her feet.

"If you're old enough to live in New York City and perform on a stage that is usually reserved for adults, then you need to be old enough to figure out how to show your brother that you can handle the grown-up pressures of living on your own. Even if you have a chaperone, me or anyone else, he has to be able to trust *you*. But I don't need to remind you that you don't have a lot of time. I'm going to go talk to Jack. Why don't you join us when you've made a decision about what to do next?"

# 12

*YOU'RE GOING to have to prove to him that you're a responsible young woman who won't be tempted to do the wrong thing just because it's easier.*

Tatiana wandered into the garden, her shoulders drooping from the weight of her own advice. In her entire four centuries of existence, Tatiana had never once felt like such a hypocrite. How could she counsel Harper about not being tempted to do the wrong thing for the sake of ease when she was doing precisely the same?

She was supposed to be granting Harper's wishes, doing everything in her human power to ensure that Jack gave his blessing to his sister's audition with the Broadway producers. She'd deluded herself in thinking that enjoying a sexual relationship with the man to soften him into changing his mind was acceptable. Because it hadn't been merely acceptable—it had been fabulous. And now, the affair was clouding her judgment. Broaching the topic of the audition with Jack was going to cause trouble, and she had been avoiding the inevitable argument the way Sleeping Beauty should have avoided that stupid spinning wheel.

Now, however, Tatiana had to make things right. She'd pulled off her conversation with Harper. Centuries as a fairy godmother had prepared her for communicating effectively with a headstrong teenager. But trying to convince a man to do something he did not want to do without a wand up her sleeve was new. And frightening.

Once upon a time, she'd pinned all her hopes and dreams

on attaining a crown by marrying a handsome, powerful prince and then serving as his queen. Yet no matter how much she'd dreamed of that outcome—no matter how she'd flirted, schemed and manipulated—she'd been denied.

She supposed this was why she understood how Harper felt about her Broadway ambitions—and why she was deathly afraid to entertain any hopes for herself beyond breaking the spell that bound her to the fairies. If she truly considered the possibility of loving Jack, marrying him, starting a family with him, would she survive if, as before, her aspirations were ripped away?

"So," Jack's voice intoned from somewhere around a blooming bush of fragrant, pink azaleas. "You've emerged from the lion's den alive."

Just the sound of his voice melted her insides. She removed her sandals and stepped off the stones that dotted the garden path, finding Jack in a favorite spot on a wicker chair that dangled from the thick branch of a live oak. Checking to make sure that any view of them from the path was blocked, she climbed onto his lap, curled against his chest and inhaled the intoxicating scent of him.

"She's really a bright girl, Jack. She's fourteen going on twenty-four."

He reached around and loosened the tie she'd used to hold her hair away from her face, then slipped his hand through the strands. "She can be twenty-four when she's twenty-four. She needs to enjoy being fourteen."

"But she's not enjoying it," she whispered.

Since she'd made her vow to Harper, Tatiana had concentrated on building Jack's trust in her at the same time as she enjoyed the perks of being his secret lover. But she had only two weeks left to change his mind about Harper's audition. She wasn't entirely certain his position was wrong, but a promise was a promise. She'd never have any future with Jack if she couldn't free herself from her fairy contract.

"She will appreciate her childhood when it's over," Jack said. "All adults do."

"Are you sure? Some kids really are destined to do more than just be kids. Some handle grown-up jobs well, with help from adults who guide them, but don't necessarily guard them."

In the light from the half moon and stars, Jack pulled back.

"Is there something you want to talk to me about?" he asked.

"I'm already talking to you about it," she replied.

He shook his head. "No, you're dancing around something. Is it the audition? Has Harper gotten to you, too?"

"Jack, I—"

But her stuttering was further interrupted by the sound of Harper calling his name.

He stood, nearly forgetting to set Tatiana on her feet before he disappeared into the garden.

"I'm here," she heard him reply.

Tatiana remained still for a minute, stunned by his abrupt departure, but not surprised. Harper was his sister. She called and he came running. Tatiana was simply a stranger he'd been sleeping with for a few weeks. A stranger whom he'd invited into his bed and into his home, but whom he hadn't made part of his decision-making process where his sister was concerned.

Jack and Harper might have gone out of their way to make her feel like family since her arrival, but boundaries still existed. Jack guarded Harper the same way another famous giant protected his treasure. And since Tatiana's relationship with Jack was based almost entirely on something as fleeting as sex, she had to tread carefully or find herself booted out the door.

Needing time to think, she put her shoes back on, pushed her way through the foliage and headed toward the dock.

A golden light shone at the point where the long, wooden structure met the land. The lamp, Jack had explained, made it easier to see the 'gators. None seemed to be hanging around the way they often did during the day, sunning themselves on the banks, so she stepped quickly onto the deck and wandered to the end. He'd warned her about not dangling her feet over the edge, so she sat on the bench instead.

Fireflies skittered over the still, dark water. Bullfrogs

squawked in the distance, the guttural sounds echoing through the mossy cypress trees and giving Tatiana a shiver. She'd run into more than a few frog princes in her life, though only one who literally fit that description. Witches changing princes into amphibians had gone out of style years ago. Frog princes nowadays were usually less-than-handsome boys who, on the outside, didn't quite measure up to some bubbleheaded princess's idea of the perfect man. But then, with a little prodding from Tatiana, the chits discovered a truly remarkable man underneath.

How lucky was she that Jack was beautiful both on the outside and the inside? And yet, she could see little hope that she'd remain in his life once she'd fulfilled Harper's wish. Unless she could somehow change his mind—and soon—making the girl's wish come true was going to mean defying him. And she was pretty certain he wasn't the forgiving type.

Not when it came to his sister.

"There you are," he said, his voice booming over the buzzing noise of the bayou.

She waved and he hopped onto the dock. His footsteps reverberated over the crackling planks, increasing the tension as he neared. She couldn't run away from this—confronting Jack about Harper's wish to sing was her only way out of her servitude. Her only way of having the future she wanted, in his world or hers.

"Why'd you disappear?" he asked.

"Harper wanted to talk to you, not to me," she replied.

He slung his hands into his pockets, a reluctantly proud grin on his face. "She apologized for the way she treated you at dinner. And for cheating on the test." He shook his head, but with a chuckle. "She said you told her she had to start acting like an adult before I could start treating her like one."

"That's not exactly what I said," Tatiana explained, though she was impressed that Harper had made the connection. "I know she's not an adult yet. But she's going to be one sooner than you think."

"I suppose my protecting her all time won't make her growing up any easier. Until now, I've never seen that as bad."

"It's not bad." Tatiana crossed her arms. The instinct to reach out and touch him was overwhelming, but she had to keep this conversation focused. "Look, I've never been a parent, but I've worked with a lot of young people and sometimes, you have to give them a chance to fail before they learn how to truly appreciate success."

"Did you ever fail? At anything big?"

Like failing to marry a prince when she'd wanted nothing else her entire life? Did that count? It wasn't as if she'd had a choice in the matter.

"I never really had much of a chance to fail."

"Overprotective parents?"

She snorted, causing them both to laugh.

"Yeah, major understatement," she explained. "But my parents weren't in my life much once I turned seventeen. I went off to school and soon after, was on my own. But I've never seriously crashed and burned, no." *Not yet, anyway.* "I guess I've been very fortunate."

He nodded, but didn't add to the conversation.

But she needed to know—wanted to know—more about what made Jack St. Cloud tick.

"What about you?" she asked.

"I crashed and burned lots of times," he said. "Mostly with Harper—trying to raise her when I was just an overgrown kid myself. My dad died just after I'd been drafted into the pros. I was living on my own, enjoying celebrity and excess during the off season and then busting my ass during training and on the field. Then Mom died. I could have been great, I guess, if I'd had more time."

"But you quit to take care of Harper," she filled in.

The idea of a brother raising his sister was very unusual. In her world, affluent parents rarely had anything to do with their offspring until they reached young adulthood. Orphans would have been looked over by regents or older, even distant, relatives before they would have been put in the care of an unmarried sibling. Even she had spent the majority of her childhood with governesses and tutors, which perhaps explained why her parents had found it so easy to give her to the fairies when their debt to the magical creatures came due.

"You could have hired a nanny or arranged for Harper to live with relatives until you were done with your career, married or settled down."

"I could have," he agreed. "That's what my agent wanted me to do. And my coaches. And my teammates. And my fiancée. But I knew it was wrong. She was only two years old and worth millions. How could I turn her over to strangers? I lived a privileged childhood. I knew what could happen to a kid who didn't have a parent in her life 24/7. It might have happened to me if I hadn't played ball. It's hard to be a spoiled brat when you're getting your brains kicked in five days a week."

A breeze stirred the air, sending her a subtle whiff of his spiced cologne. Unable to resist touching him any longer, she smoothed his dark hair away from his forehead. "I'm glad your brains survived."

"Does that mean you think I'm right to keep Harper away from Broadway?"

She pressed her lips together tightly. It was now or never. If she kept running away from this conversation or losing herself in the sexual and emotional delight of being Jack's lover, she'd never be free to take their relationship to the next level.

"I think Harper has a fabulous talent," she admitted after a deep breath. "And I think she has an amazing desire to share that talent with the world. Her ambition is very real and very sincere. But mostly, I think she feels like she's wasting away here. I also think that she loves you very deeply and she desperately wants your approval. Her singing voice connects her to her mother, but you connect her to her father. Keeping her away from that audition and withholding your approval, to her, is like erasing your mother and father from her memory."

As she feared, with each word she spoke, Jack's eyes grew

darker and harder. His jaw set in such a way that she knew he was clenching his teeth. After a thick swallow, he stood.

"Wow," he said.

"I know that's a lot to take in—" she began, but he held up his hand to stop her.

"It is. You've clearly thought a lot about my sister. And I appreciate your opinion," he said, but Tatiana could hear the distinct sound of forced politeness in his tone. "I'm glad you came here and that you're helping Harper with school, but I can't allow you to encourage false hopes. I watched that industry drain my father and kill my mother. I won't allow the insanity and fickle nature of fame destroy my sister, too. If she's as talented as you believe, she can wait until she's mature enough to handle the pressure and the temptation."

More than anything in the world, Tatiana wanted to take the word *temptation* and turn it into some kind of sexy innuendo that would spin the conversation away from Harper and repair what she suspected was a widening rift between her and Jack. But she couldn't. The clock was ticking. Her time to be free, to spread her wings rather than wear them, was running out.

"You asked my opinion, Jack," she said, a bit more snap in her voice than was likely prudent. "Or did you only want to hear from me if I agreed with you?"

He shoved his hands into his pockets. "You aren't responsible for her, I am. I can't only think about what's best for Harper *now*. I have to think about what's best for the rest of her life."

"And what about what's best for you?"

"I don't matter," he said flippantly.

"You matter to me," she argued.

"Well, I shouldn't. If I have to choose between Harper's future happiness and mine, then I choose hers."

"Why can't you choose both?"

His jaw twitched. He wanted to say something more. She could see it in his eyes. But instead, he broke his stare with her, focusing instead into the dark bayou behind them. "I don't know how. Do you? Have you discovered the secret to making everyone in your life happy, including yourself?"

Tatiana didn't reply. The only secret she knew—that she had to convince him to allow Harper to audition in order to ensure her freedom from her bonds as a fairy godmother— would rip their tentative relationship apart.

He'd never believe her if she told him the truth. She had no means to prove her claims. No wand to show him. No wings. He'd write her off as a crazy woman and send her packing before she could corrupt his sister further.

But if she proceeded to press him about allowing Harper's audition, he was going to tune her out. He was doing it right now, his gaze barely meeting hers simply because she'd expressed a solicited opinion that contradicted his.

She swallowed a gasp, realizing she had no other choice. In order to grant Harper's wish, she was going to have to go against everything Jack believed—everything he'd sacrificed his personal happiness for.

In other words, she was going to have to break his trust— and possibly, his heart.

# 13

FOR THE next week, Ana found excuses to leave the house during the afternoons. Once, she claimed she needed Mrs. Bradley to drive her into town to shop for personal items and refused Jack's offer to take her himself. Another time, she made arrangements with Harper's French teacher to review the curriculum for her tutoring. The next day, she simply walked out into the bayou before lunch and returned hours later, flowers in her hair, sweaty, bug-bitten and beautiful. Jack might have joined her for the shower she insisted she needed if Harper hadn't arrived home early, snagging Ana for herself so they could go over some particularly troublesome conjugations. By Friday, Jack had become accustomed to having Ana in the house without having her in his bed.

He'd tried to appreciate having his privacy back, but every time he thought about her, his body thrummed and his pulse beat as if he'd grown a second heart. He missed her. But their disagreement over Harper's future had dug a chasm between them that he wasn't sure either of them could bridge.

She meant well, he knew, but he'd been Harper's only parent for twelve years. He'd sacrificed his football career to keep her safe from any number of threats—distant relatives who wanted access to her inheritance, the press who wanted to exploit the poor little heiress and the ambitions that could drive her down that same destructive road as their mother. He couldn't stop protecting Harper just because it was more convenient to his love life.

Though since he'd made his choice, he no longer had a love life.

All he had were several lazy hours worth of erotic memories, which he replayed in his mind more and more frequently as the week came to a close.

On Saturday, he threw himself completely into his work. He spent six solid hours fielding e-mails, making phone calls, trading stocks and increasing the portfolios of several of his clients. In the afternoon, he paused near the intercom, tempted to discover what Ana and Harper were doing, but stalked into his studio and painted until sunset instead.

Only after his stomach growled did he realize that no one had called him for dinner.

He descended into the kitchen and the silence in the house gave a hollow sound to his footsteps. He shouted for Mrs. Bradley, but she didn't answer. He'd already checked Harper's bedroom and found it empty. The guest room, where Ana had insisted on staying (and which she and Harper had cleaned up and decorated with some of the more sparkly props and costumes from his mother's collection), proved unoccupied, as well.

He checked his cell phone, which he'd turned off while he was painting. He had a text message from Harper.

The first message read: Went shopping. The second, sent several hours later: Car broke down. At the Boudreaux place. Pick us up!

The Boudreaux family lived closer to Hastings than Jack did, but their cabin was small and without running water. From what little he knew of his neighbors, they didn't take to visitors. Cursing for losing himself in his art—which had grown more and more erotic the longer he and Ana were apart—he punched in a response for them to stay put, grabbed the keys to his truck and headed out to rescue them from a dinner of stewed possum and dirty rice, whose name might not be as metaphoric as the usual Cajun-style recipe.

Unlike his house, which he'd built on stilts and flooded

with light to keep the creatures away at nighttime, the Boudreauxs' house sat like a toad, squat and hunched amid the cypress trees that nearly blocked it from view. Once he'd fought his way over the marshy path that led to the cabin, the sound of singing greeted him. Quite a few animals slithered or skittered out of his way as he marched up to the porch. A single oil lamp burned by the door, but bright golden light poured out of the window along with the music.

The sound was angelic. Not one voice, but two—intertwined and harmonious—with one soaring into the high notes, the other belting out the low. Through a slit in the dingy curtains, he spied Ana and Harper standing across from the Boudreaux family and Mrs. Bradley, singing a show tune once performed by his mother and her best friend. The same best friend who had been at her side when Marina St. Cloud ingested one too many hits of cocaine. The same best friend who had called for help while his mother's body cried uncle.

He banged loudly on the door.

From inside, Ana yelped in surprise. Harper's voice on the other hand, continued for a few more notes, as if she'd been so wrapped up in the song even the booming sound of Jack's fist against the rotting wood couldn't pull her from her performance.

"Who's there?" asked a gruff male voice.

"Jack St. Cloud," he replied.

The door flew open. Paul Boudreaux was a small, wiry man with a gap-toothed smile. "Come on in! Your sister and her friend were just giving us a concert. Beautiful voices. Straight from above. Come on in and give a listen."

Jack lingered on the other side of the threshold. Mr. Boudreaux slid out of the way to allow Jack room to enter, but the minute he caught sight of Ana's and Harper's faces, he could not move. His sister's expression was one of shock and fear. Ana's reflected guilt and not a little defiance. It was only then that he realized the two women could not have performed so flawlessly on a whim.

They'd been rehearsing.

"I'm sorry, Mr. Boudreaux. I certainly don't mean to be rude, but the women of my household have imposed on you and your family long enough. I think it's time we got going."

Contradicting Jack's perception of the neighbors he'd lived near for twelve years, Mr. Boudreaux proved friendly and gregarious, refusing Jack's notion that they could depart without first sharing some of the homemade biscuits his plump wife had just drawn out of their woodburning stove. They gathered around a pocked and dented table and slathered the pillows of deliciousness in honey that one of the Boudreaux children had harvested from a hive in the bayou while Mr. Boudreaux took out his fiddle and played.

By the time he'd pulled out a jug of something he called Bayou Moon for the adults (which smelled suspiciously like high-octane gasoline) and his wife had poured lemonade for the younger set, Jack was more than ready to leave. He and Ana had some serious talking to do—and it was far past Harper's bedtime. But now that he knew how nice his neighbors were, he decided they should stay long enough for everyone to finish their drinks.

Ana, apparently, was smart enough not to do anything more than politely sip the strangely golden liquid in her mason jar, but Mrs. Bradley took a mouthful and declared it surprisingly smooth. That caused Paul Boudreaux to pour twice as much in the woman's glass, ensuring they'd be stuck here a little while longer.

Jack wandered out onto the porch while Harper begged Mr. Boudreaux to show her how to properly hold a fiddle.

Ana joined him a few minutes later.

"I can't believe you rehearsed with her," he said, suddenly not so adverse to drinking Mr. Boudreaux's home brew. Mrs. Bradley hadn't been off base. The stuff was potent, but went down like single malt, despite the fact that his stomach was churning with acid.

"Oh, is there a rule against that, too?" Ana asked, defiantly.

"Maybe you should be a little more specific about the things I'm allowed to do with your sister."

"I told you I don't want you to encourage her," he said.

"Someone has to," Ana snapped.

"Why? She knows she's talented. Why does the whole damned world have to know?"

"Because she wants the world to know, Jack." Ana cursed, then moved closer. He could feel her hand hovering near his arm, as if she wanted to touch him, but was afraid.

Almost unconsciously, he leaned back so that her fingers brushed against his sleeve. The sensation hinted at warmth, but was not powerful enough to shatter the cold wall between them.

"I don't want to fight with you," she admitted. "I miss you."

He turned and in the darkness of the porch, slid his hands around her waist. "I didn't ask you to stay away. I miss you, too. I don't want this to come between us."

She nodded, but did not reply. Not that he gave her much of a chance, since he lowered his head and stole a kiss. It was quick, but incendiary. Blood rushed from his brain to his groin, making him dizzy, making him hot. He'd never have a moment's peace until he buried himself in Ana's softness and lost himself in the delirium of her passion. Her breasts brushed his chest and the beads of her nipples told him she wasn't unaffected by him, either.

"Ana?"

The sound of Harper's voice made them separate quickly. A split second later, the girl opened the door. "Mr. Boudreaux taught me to pluck the fiddle. Wanna hear?"

Ana's hand instinctively covered her lips. Jack hoped his sister wouldn't spy the tenderness of her tutor's flesh, the blush on her cheeks or the guilty look in her eyes.

"Sure, hon," Ana answered, "but then we have to go. It's late and your brother has been waiting long enough."

She disappeared inside. Yeah, Jack had been waiting a long time for Ana. A whole damned week. Maybe his whole life.

# 14

THE RIDE home was relatively quiet, though Mrs. Bradley was more talkative than usual. Tatiana suspected the housekeeper had had more of Mr. Boudreaux's Bayou Moon liquor than she was going to be happy about in the morning. Once they arrived back at the house, Harper helped the older woman to her room and put her to bed, while Jack disappeared into his study. Tatiana waited until she heard Harper go upstairs before she knocked and then opened Jack's door.

The study was dark, except for the slightly bluish glow from his computer screen. Jack's face, illuminated by the screen, was shadowed. He spared her a glance, then returned to listening to his messages on his speaker phone while scrolling through what she assumed were e-mails. She'd watched him work before, usually while waiting until he could take her to his bedroom and while away the remaining daytime hours in more pleasurable pursuits.

Suddenly, the memory of his fingering her to orgasm while he suckled her breasts mercilessly sprung into her mind. Deciding that talking to him tonight was not a good idea, she turned to leave. But as her hand touched the door latch, one of the messages caught her ear.

"Mr. St. Cloud, this is David Lucas again. I hate to keep bothering you, but my partner and I are only going to be in New Orleans for another couple of days. We're staying at the Hotel Monteleone and we're holding auditions at the Saenger. To be honest, we only opened auditions to give us something to do. We really just want to hear Harper. And, of course, to discuss concerns you might have about our production. I knew your mother, Mr. St. Cloud. I understand your concerns for Harper's well-being, but I assure you, we can make all the necessary arrangements for chaperones—"

Jack clicked off the phone.

Tatiana stared at him. "They've been contacting you?"

Jack grabbed a stack of papers and gave them an unnecessary and rough straightening. "Two or three calls a day for over a week. Broadway producers don't like taking no for an answer."

"That must mean they really want Harper to audition."

He scoffed. "She could sing like a toad and they'd hire her for the publicity alone."

"But she doesn't sing like a toad," Tatiana argued. "She sings like an ang—"

"Yeah, an angel. I know. I heard you. I heard *both* of you."

He took a deep breath and Tatiana could tell he was trying to rein in his emotions—anger first and foremost. "I can't argue about this with you anymore, Ana. You simply have to accept my decision."

"Why? Because I'm just a stranger who came into your life accidentally? Because I'm just some woman you've been making love with to pass the time?"

"No." He slammed his hands on the desk and stood. "You're more than that to me."

"But not enough to influence how you treat your sister, a young girl that I care about deeply."

He grabbed the sides of his head. "Enough! My decision is made."

The finality in his voice nearly snapped her in two. The producers were only in town for a couple of more days, so her timeline for fulfilling Harper's wish and winning her own freedom had just shrunk to nearly nothing. She'd been rehearsing with Harper on the sly, hoping to show Jack just how spectacularly talented his sister was and convince him to, at the very least, allow her to gain the experience of a professional audition. But now her plan was falling apart.

"Jack, please. Just let her audition. Give her your blessing. She doesn't have to take the role if they offer it to her. But it means so much to her to try out." *So much to me.* "Then, I swear, we'll have everything we've ever wanted."

Jack refused. "You want me to let her get her hopes up and then rip the carpet out from under her? That's cruel. Believe me, they'll want her and Harper won't be able to resist. Then I'm going to have to tell her no all over again."

He was right, of course, but what else could Tatiana do? If Harper did not audition with Jack's blessing, Tatiana would have to return to Elatyria forever. Joe Stiltskin had warned her, though at the time, his caveat had meant nothing to her. She'd expected to come into this world, fulfill the wish of a human girl without magic and break her unwanted bond. She hadn't thought about what she'd do afterward, though the idea of seeking out a prince and resuming her quest for the throne had not entirely left her.

But she'd never anticipated meeting a man like Jack. Never guessed she'd fall so hard that her insides coiled at the idea of losing him forever. Because if she failed, not only would she serve the rest of her long life as a fairy godmother, she'd forget him. She'd have no memory of the intimacies they'd shared or the powerful secrets she'd learned about herself in his arms.

"You're the most stubborn man I've ever met," she said, her voice rising.

"Stubborn?" he said, coming around the desk. "You think my pride drives this decision?"

"No," she conceded. "I understand why you're afraid for Harper, I honestly do. But if you only knew everything that is riding on this, you wouldn't be so inflexible."

"Riding?" He took a step back and swallowed thickly. His eyes first widened in shock, and then narrowed. "Ana, please don't tell me you work for David Lucas. Swear to me he didn't send you here to soften the way to Harper's audition."

The betrayal in his stare sliced her to her core, but would

not prove half as eviscerating as his reaction when she told
him the truth. "No one sent me here. I came here on my own."

"For Harper?"

She shook her head. "For myself."

"What are you talking about?"

Suddenly, the study walls seemed confining, as if they were
closing in. She had no choice. She had to tell him the truth.

"Not here." She took his hand and tugged, wanting him to
leave with her.

"What? Ana, wait."

But she didn't hesitate and luckily, he didn't resist. She
pulled him out of the study, through the house and out the
front door, snagging the flashlight he kept on the porch and
flicking on the beam. Once they reached the bottom of the
steps, he tried to stop her, but she let go of his hand and broke
into a run, only realizing that tears were streaming down her
face when she could hardly see her way to the edge of the
trees where she'd first emerged with Harper.

He overtook her, braced her shoulders and held her still.
"Ana, tell me what's wrong."

"My name isn't Ana. It's Tatiana. Tatiana Starlingham.
I'm not who you think I am."

"You're not a French tutor?"

She laughed, but the sound was hollow and tragic, even to
her own ears. "I'm not anything in your world, this world.
When I said I wasn't from here, I wasn't kidding. I'm from
another place, a place you don't even believe in—or at least,
a place you haven't believed in since you were a child. A place
where wishes come true because fair—er, people like me
make them come true. With magic and wands and wings. I
belong in a place where your fairy tales come from, a place
you can't find except during a full moon somewhere south of
here, where the walls between your world and mine blur.
That's how I got here, hoping to find a way to free myself
from a pact my parents made when I was barely older than
Harper. She made a wish, Jack. Harper did. She wished to

audition for the role, but with your approval and support. I can't use magic to grant her wish. I have to use you. And if you don't give Harper your blessing and take her to that audition, I have to go back to my world forever."

Fueled by her desperation to make him understand, she took his hand again and pulled him to the clearing where she and Harper had first met, well aware that he was coming along only because she'd shocked him into submission.

When they reached the clearing, she stopped and looked up into the sky, trying to chart the direction of the portal to Elatyria from the position of the stars. But the moon caught her eye first. It was a half-moon—days away from the waning full that would force her return home.

Only she didn't want to go home. She wanted her bond broken, yes, but she wanted to stay here, with Jack. And Harper. And Mrs. Bradley. And the Boudreaux family down the way. And the hamlet of Hastings and the city of New Orleans and the state of Louisiana. She loved everything about being here.

But mostly, she loved Jack.

Yet when she turned to face him, she saw nothing but confusion and fear in the hypnotic brown eyes she adored so desperately.

"I haven't lost my mind," she assured him.

"Really? Because I think you just told me that you come from some kind of alternate universe."

"That's one way to put it," she conceded.

Jack's face paled to the same gray whiteness as the surface of the moon that ruled her passage.

"Ana, are you playing some sort of game?"

She threw her arms around his neck and kissed him. She hadn't planned to, but she'd always been smarter than most—she knew she was seconds away from losing him forever. She had to take this now. It might be her last kiss before her whole world spun out of control.

He did not respond, but instead pushed her away. "This isn't funny."

She stumbled, but did not fall. "It's not a game. It's not a joke. I have absolutely no way to convince you that what I'm saying is true, but you have to believe me when I say it is. You have to give Harper your blessing to audition or by Friday, I'll have to return to where I came from and I won't be able to come back. Ever."

Jack turned and stalked twelve paces in the other direction before he whirled and stabbed an angry finger in her direction. "You're just like all the rest. Trying to get something from me. Something from Harper. I don't know exactly what you want, but I'm not giving you a chance to take it before I can stop you. You stay away from my sister. You stay away from me. I'm not going to leave you out here in the middle of the night, but you go back to the house, stay in your room until morning and then I'll drive you…somewhere. Anywhere. I can't believe I was so stupid that I let you into my life. You're nuts."

She held her tongue, afraid of what might come out of her mouth if she opened it. She was furious. She was heartbroken. She was angry that he didn't believe her, even though she knew that no rational man from this world ever could. She'd never planned to tell him the truth. She'd hoped to arrange the audition, gain her freedom and then continue to live with him and his family for the rest of her life—though she hadn't realized until this moment that she had such a specific plan at all.

He didn't leave right away, but stared at her long and hard, as if willing her to take back all the crazy things she'd claimed.

But she couldn't.

She couldn't deny the truth—just as she couldn't deny that what she'd feared had come to pass. Jack no longer wanted anything to do with her and Harper had no chance of auditioning.

Finally, he walked away. Tatiana, however, did not follow. She didn't have the strength. Instead, she dropped to the ground and surrendered to the tears burning behind her eyes. The last one didn't drop until the sun broke over the distant horizon.

# 15

"IF YOU'RE looking for Ana, she's gone," Harper said, snapping at Jack when he emerged from the house just before noon. She halted her march across the hardwood planks on the porch and waved Ana's cryptic note at him. "What did you do to her?"

Jack crossed his arms, looking every bit the imposing giant she'd often imagined him to be. Well, she was done listening to him, bowing to his proclamations and edicts as if he were some sort of king. Or her father. He wasn't either. He was her brother and he'd not only taken away her opportunity to follow her mother's legacy and sing on the stage, but he'd taken away the only woman who'd ever believed in her talent as much as she did.

"I didn't do anything to her," he replied, his voice raspy. "I don't think she was entirely…stable."

"Why? Because she thought I had talent? Because she believed in me? Because she had the guts to stand up to you and tell you you're an overbearing, overprotective asshole who's so afraid of living his own life, he won't let his sister live hers?"

Harper gasped for breath and turned away. Wow. She hadn't meant to say all that, but she meant every word. She knew how her mother had died—knew more details than Jack had ever told her. She wasn't stupid.

"I'm not afraid for myself," Jack insisted. "But yeah, I'm scared as hell for you."

Harper ran her hand through her hair and down her face,

surprised that she wasn't crying. She was beyond tears, she supposed, having cried most of them out when she'd first read Ana's letter, informing her about how to get in touch with the producers at the Hotel Monteleone and encouraging her to try and convince Jack on her own since Ana had not only failed to sway her immovable brother, but she'd somehow completely broken his trust in some unfixable way. Harper didn't understand adults. If they made all of the decisions, why couldn't they fix all of their mistakes?

"Then come with me," she offered. "Come with me to New Orleans and if I pass the test, come with me to New York. You can work anywhere. Hasn't it ever occurred to you to leave? Or do you prefer the swamp? Living far away from the real world? Would you rather stay up in that studio of yours and paint sexy portraits instead of, I don't know, actually having sex with a hot woman like Ana?"

She knew she'd said too much the minute Jack's face turned from fuchsia to red to nearly purple. Scared, she ran forward and punched him in the chest, reminding him to breathe.

He staggered backward. "You're way out of line, little sister."

Jack wasn't going to drop dead like her father. He was strong and healthy, even if he was more stubborn than a mule. She took a deep breath and decided to go for broke.

"No, I'm not. First, yes, I've been in your studio. Many times. But I've never seen you paint anything so sensual until Ana came around. So, yes, I know you're in serious lust with Ana. Who wouldn't be? She's a knockout. Besides, I saw you kiss her last night on the Boudreauxs' porch, and though I haven't seen many real-life kisses, it certainly didn't look like your first one. It's about time you got your game on again. I'm happy for you."

"I'm not talking about this with you," he insisted.

"Right," Harper said. "And who else do you have to discuss it with?"

As if caught by some sort of magic spell, Jack walked to the edge of the porch and sat on the top step. He leaned his elbows on his knees and put his head down.

Finally. She'd never seen her brother beaten before, but she imagined this is what he'd looked like the few times on the sidelines when his team had not come out victorious. Defeat didn't look so bad on him, really.

She joined him and put her hand on his shoulder. "You're a big guy, Jack. Big and stupid."

"Thanks," he muttered.

"If you can't rely on your little sister to tell you the truth, then you can't rely on anyone."

He turned his head to the side without sitting up. "You really saw my paintings?"

She blushed and shivered. "Yeah, but to be honest, I'd rather not talk about it."

"Fine with me."

"But I do want to talk about Ana."

That put him bolt upright. "Not so fine with me."

"You could love her, Jack. She's smart and creative and wise and beautiful and—"

"Crazy," he supplied.

Harper shrugged. "Nobody's perfect. But she believed in me, Jack. She believed in us. The whole time she was helping me with my audition, she said over and over that you needed to approve. I even wanted to go behind your back, but she said she'd done that enough just by helping me practice. She reminded me that from the very beginning, I've wanted to do this with your approval. She's right. I can't do this without you. But Jack, I really, really need to see if I've got the stuff to make it on Broadway without self-destructing. Mom couldn't. But Mom didn't have you watching her back."

Jack's eyes grew glossy and Harper pressed her forehead against his bicep, determined not to look at him if he was going to finally let loose after all these years. She might have cried herself out earlier, but she'd find a renewed store if her brother lost it.

"You really want to leave all this? Leave your childhood behind and go to New York?"

"I just want to go to New Orleans first and try. Maybe they won't even like me."

He wrapped his big, strong arm around her shoulder and pulled her in close. "Are you kidding me? They're going to love you. You're fabulous."

"You really think so?"

"I haven't told you, and that was wrong. But you're more talented than Mom ever was. And you've got a better head on your shoulders. And you're right, you have me. Where you go, I go, kid."

Harper jumped to her feet and squealed so loudly, she thought she might have damaged her vocal chords. She clamped her hand over her mouth and did a little marching dance on the balls of her feet instead.

Jack laughed. When she finally took her hand away, she whispered, "Then I can do it? I can audition?"

He stood and wrapped her in his arms. "Yes."

"I've got to tell Ana!"

"Now, Harper," he said warningly. "I still think she's lost her mind."

"I don't care if she escaped from a mental ward, I need her. She's my good-luck charm. I'm going inside to call the producers and set up an appointment!"

Harper heard Jack start to argue, but she didn't stick around. Whatever his objections were, she didn't care.

Ana had done what she'd promised—she'd made Harper's wish come true. Trouble was, unless Jack tracked her down, she might never know.

For the second time, Jack was drawn to his sister's location by the sound of her voice. A stale-water smell, not unlike the bayou, greeted him as he pushed inside the old Saenger Theater. Not yet under renovations since sustaining serious damage from Hurricane Katrina, the old structure appeared barely safe. The walls were mottled and chipped from the water damage and the once-bright and brilliant paint on the bas-reliefs had peeled and faded to a shade somewhere between beige and gray.

But the acoustics, apparently, were unharmed. Harper's voice echoed through the emptiness, haunting and powerful. Her every word and enunciation was crisp and clear, despite the fact that he was in the lobby of the old movie house and she was on stage, a beautiful, fresh flower amidst the wilting decay of the theater.

He'd spent all morning trying to fulfill the promise he'd made to find Ana. Rather, Tatiana. Tatiana Starlingham, a woman Sean Devlin assured him had no birth certificate, no passport, no driver's license, no green card—nothing to prove she'd ever lived anywhere in this world.

He'd enlisted the private investigator's help, but Ana had disappeared like a whiff of smoke. He and Sean had searched every room in the bayou house and the grounds for clues to where Ana might have gone, but they'd come up empty. Jack had had no choice but to leave for New Orleans so he didn't miss the audition that fulfilled his sister's lifelong dream.

He'd been so angry and confused last night. If only he'd listened more closely. Asked more questions. But he'd surrendered to fear and anger and had likely destroyed any chance he'd ever have at winning back a woman who might be insane, but who had definitely found a way into his heart.

The plush red velvet seats that had filled the auditorium before the flood had been removed, so five folding chairs were lined across the slanted floor, each occupied by, Jack assumed, the Broadway producers. The theater still didn't have electricity and the stifling heat had caused two of the men in the group to remove their jackets and the third to lean forward as if he was about to melt on the spot. Mrs. Bradley, who had driven Harper into the city, sat in the center seat. The fifth seat, he assumed, was for him.

Harper's gaze met his and with a tentative step forward, she continued her a cappella performance of a song their mother had once sung in a performance of *On a Clear Day, You Can See Forever.*

He'd heard the lyrics a hundred times. His mother had often sung it to him as a lullaby. He'd even seen Streisand interpret the song on film, and yet, Harper took the music to a new level. She'd added a bluesy swagger, and as she approached the big finish, her voice rose to octaves he wasn't sure he'd heard her hit before. The producers had literally shifted to the edges of their seats. Mrs. Bradley was weeping with pride.

For his part, Jack couldn't move. The desperation in Harper's lyrical question echoed throughout the cavernous theater. A woman wondered why she couldn't win back her lover's love—questioned what she'd lost that he'd once found so irresistible. If only Jack had found Ana, he'd have what he'd never had before—a sister who had just run for a game-winning touchdown and a woman he could love.

He clapped first and loudest, even adding a whistle that probably made every dog in the Quarter run toward the theater. Harper beamed with pleasure, ignoring the producers entirely—her eyes were trained only on him. After a few seconds elapsed, her smile disappeared. She'd realized that he was alone.

Unfortunately, he'd taken a lot longer to figure out just how alone he'd been—too long to win Ana back.

# 16

HARPER and Mrs. Bradley watched from the truck as Jack lifted his fist to knock on the Boudreauxs' door. By the time he'd discussed all the details regarding Harper's debut in the Broadway revival of *Once Upon a Mattress,* the group had been together for hours. Though he'd desperately wanted to resume his search for Ana, he couldn't politely refuse the producers' invitation to dinner to celebrate.

He'd been firm in his negotiation of terms, and the producers had agreed to everything—including paying for a full-time tutor of Harper's choosing. Jack could have afforded this, of course, but the only tutor Harper wanted— Tatiana Starlingham—was someone he didn't want as his employee.

He wanted her as a lover. A partner. A friend. Unfortunately, Jack didn't have a clue where to find her.

It was Mrs. Bradley's suggestion that they contact the Boudreaux family, since they were the only other people Ana had spent time with during her brief stay. Paul must have heard them drive up because he opened the door before Jack could touch the splintered wood with his knuckles.

"Knew you'd show up here," he said, rubbing his stubbled chin with bemusement.

"Excuse me?" Jack asked.

"Looking for that pretty lady that was here last night, are you?"

Jack's chest tightened. "Have you seen her?"

"Sure I seen her. She showed up here early this morning,

all torn up." Paul Boudreaux puffed up his lean chest, attempting, Jack supposed, to match him in size. Well, that wasn't going to happen, but the censure in the man's piercing eyes was still powerful and effective. "I suppose you think you're some sort of big man, breaking her heart, huh?"

"No, sir," Jack replied. "We just had a misunderstanding. I need to find her and tell her I believe her."

Jack didn't know where that came from. Ana had been talking gibberish during her big confession, and while he'd tried to rationalize that her sudden bout of insanity had been brought on by extreme pressure from their argument over his sister, he hadn't quite managed to buy that explanation. And yet, she'd been right about Harper. She'd been right about him. He hadn't been hiding only his sister in the bayou—he'd been hiding himself.

"You believe that she's a fairy godmother trying to work her way out of the fairy-tale world?" Boudreaux asked, eyebrow arched.

Jack blinked. He hadn't imagined she'd share that nutty story with anyone else.

"Um, yeah?" he answered tentatively.

Fairy godmother? Okay, now Jack really had stepped into the Twilight Zone. Especially since Boudreaux looked like this declaration was no different from Jack claiming that he used to play for the New York Giants—which he had.

Boudreaux laughed and slapped him on the back. "You're smarter than you look, boy. Crazy story, I know, but there are stranger things happening here in the bayou, that's for sure. Take your womenfolk back home and get them tucked into bed. Then come back here and I'll tell you the rest of her story. She spilled her guts to the lot of us. Poor child. She's crazy in love with you. At least she was. Now that she's back in that weird world o' hers, she won't remember a thing about you."

"Won't remember?"

Boudreaux grabbed his arm and, for a little guy, had a surprising amount of strength as he pushed Jack off the porch. "Go on now. When you get back, I'll help you find her."

"Find her? You know where she went?"

"Yes, sir. She went home," Boudreaux replied, casting an enigmatic glance into the darkness. "Luckily for you, son, I know where that is."

*No CHEMISTRY.*

Tatiana yawned, not bothering to cover her mouth. Since she'd returned to Elatyria, she hadn't gotten enough sleep. She needed to talk to the fairy council about replacing her bed. Honestly, who could expect even an enchanted mattress to last four centuries?

"Okay, enough!" she said.

The prince and princess huddled in conversation on a gilded settee across from her broke apart. The girl, poor dear, looked utterly confused. But the prince's expression communicated a clear and righteous, "I told you so."

She floated over to the princess, whose pretty green eyes were glossy and, bless her, a little vacant. "It's not you, dear. It's him."

"Wh-what?"

A single tear slid down the girl's cheek. Very convincing, this one. Probably thought her whole world was going to fall apart if she didn't get a marriage proposal from Prince Ruprecht this very evening. But it obviously wasn't going to happen. While Ruprecht wouldn't confess, Tatiana suspected he had someone else on his mind. Probably a commoner of some sort. His royal mother clearly possessed great influence and power if she'd convinced the fairy council to grant a godmother to a prince. In all her many lifetimes, Tatiana had never served the male side of the royal equation before.

She patted the princess's shoulder gently. "Okay, how do I put this? He's just not that into you."

From the girl's confounded expression, Tatiana realized that the phraseology she'd picked up somewhere (she couldn't quite remember where) had no effect—and she could see why. In Elatyria, dreams and wishes came true on a regular basis. Princesses such as this one had been raised to be wholly unprepared for disappointment. Well, that was *her* fairy godmother's problem. On this case, Tatiana was working for the other team.

Tatiana flicked her wrist and her wand appeared. She waved the star-topped baton around the girl's head, creating a sparkly mist that engulfed her head. "You're going back to your kingdom now. You'll forget all about Prince Ruprecht. Study French. It'll improve your vocabulary," she proclaimed, and then, with a second flick, the princess disappeared.

"Thank you!" Ruprecht said, throwing himself back dramatically.

Tatiana tilted an eyebrow. Why so many princesses wanted to fall into bed with this joker was beyond her. He was cute, she supposed, and not as anxious as some of the other princes she'd met to bed his prospective wives before he declared them unsuitable for one stupid reason or another. In fact, the guy seemed utterly disinterested in women all together. He'd even been unimpressed by her. While she couldn't remember noticing before, Tatiana now realized that she was hot. She had not been aware of her own attractiveness for a very long time and couldn't quite put her finger on why that had changed.

It certainly wasn't because of any reaction on Ruprecht's part. He probably wouldn't notice if she had a wardrobe malfunction and flashed a breast or two. At least this explained why the queen had called in the big guns.

Only, Tatiana wasn't feeling much like an omnipotent expert on matters of the heart at the moment.

"Are we through here?" she asked.

"Please!" Ruprecht replied. "I told you she was all wrong for me."

Tatiana floated to the settee and sat beside him.

"You had no chemistry," she concluded.

"You're telling me. But how do you know about chemistry, anyway? I thought fairy godmothers weren't allowed to experience feelings of passion."

"How do you know that?"

The rules of the fairy world weren't exactly common knowledge.

He shrugged, the gilded epaulet on his shoulder brushing against a surprisingly smooth and pale cheek. "I had a very unhealthy interest in fairies when I was younger."

"Okay," Tatiana said. "I'm so outta here. I'll come back when I've found another princess for you to reject."

"That's the spirit!" he said, sarcasm ringing.

She liked Prince Ruprecht. Liked him a lot—in a friendly sort of way. He was funny, handsome, quick-witted and completely disinterested in choosing a wife. Sounded an awful lot like a man she once knew, a man who was haunting her dreams—but one she couldn't quite identify. Only this man was large and tough and—

The door to Prince Ruprecht's room burst open. A hulk of a man tore inside, slammed the entry closed and slid the cross bar into place.

"Finally!" he said, staring directly at Tatiana.

She met his rich, dark-chocolate gaze and for a brief moment, her entire body tingled.

"Who are you?" she asked, brandishing her wand at him.

The dark-haired man the size of three Ruprechts made eye contact with the prince. For a moment, the royal's gaze darkened with interest unlike any she had seen in him before. But then he frowned and sighed.

"All the good ones are taken," the prince declared, then stood wearily. "I suppose you want me to disappear?"

"If you would, your highness," the stranger answered, a bit of a stutter in his voice, before he managed a wholly unpracticed bow.

"No problem," he said.

"Don't you dare!" Tatiana declared. "I don't know who this man is or why he's here!"

"Unfortunately," Ruprecht said, "he's not here for me. Go with the flow, Tatiana. At least you might end up the one having *your* dreams fulfilled tonight."

Ruprecht ended his confusing statement with a saucy wink, then approached the stranger, whispered something in his ear and disappeared into an antechamber hidden behind a tapestry, leaving her locked in with this towering, exceedingly handsome man.

Well, not literally *locked in*. She could poof herself out if she wanted to.

But strangely, she didn't want to.

"Who are you?" she asked again.

He took a step nearer, but she poked her wand forward, stopping him. "My name is Jack St. Cloud."

Jack? Jack St. Cloud? Was that supposed to mean something to her? She supposed it should, judging by the expectant look he gave her. But while the name didn't sound completely foreign, she couldn't quite place it, either.

"You don't remember?" he asked.

"No, I don't. I mean, not really."

A grin spread across his face that was nothing short of devastating. She couldn't resist lowering her wand. He seemed so pleased by the fact that she had not dismissed him outright. Something about him was familiar. Deeply familiar. Sensations not unlike a fizzing of magic skittered over her skin.

"Are you a wizard of some sort?" she asked.

"No," he replied, stepping nearer.

This time, she allowed it.

"I'm just a man. Boudreaux warned me that you might not remember who I was, that once you stepped back into this world, your memories of the other would fade."

"Other?"

He closed in on her, but instead of feeling threatened or alarmed, her entire body was engulfed in warmth. She was suddenly aware that she was hovering with anticipation, so she fluttered to the ground.

She landed unsteadily and the stranger took the opportunity to catch her by the arms.

"Let me go," she said, unconvincingly.

"I can't."

"Why not?"

"Because I love you," he said. "And you love me."

"I don't know you."

"Give me a second to reintroduce myself."

And he kissed her. He tugged her forward and pressed his mouth against hers. The flavors were intriguing and she didn't fight when he coaxed her mouth open with his tongue. Flesh to flesh, something stirred within her—but she wasn't sure it was any sort of recollection. It was more like a fire deep in her belly. Maybe deeper. Like her soul.

"Now do you remember?" he asked, though he'd barely broken away and his words were like another layer of kisses against her lips.

"Not really," she said.

He took her wand from her hand and flung it onto the settee. Then he hooked one arm around her waist, slipped the other behind her neck and pressed her whole body tight to his. He kissed her again, this time with just enough savagery to burn away the fog that kept her from placing precisely how she knew how to hold him, how to touch him, how to respond to the blaze that now burned full-force within her.

Jack.

Suddenly, her body felt heavier. Out of the corner of her eye, she caught the sparkle and flash of her wand going up in flames. Yeah, she knew how it felt. She was about to burn from the inside out because Jack St. Cloud had come for her.

She wrapped her leg around his calf and pressed tighter, reveling in the feel of his erection against her. Yes! She remembered everything! Her decision to cross out of this world. Meeting Harper. Catching sight of Jack. Learning about the joys of sex and intimacy first on her own and then, gloriously, with him. But when she remembered their fight over Harper's future, and her desperation for him to understand why she'd contradicted him, she pulled away.

She'd run from him. She'd chosen to return to her servitude as a fairy godmother rather than deal with the heartbreak. Her abject sorrow had allowed her to return to Elatyria even though the moon cycle was wrong—a secret she'd learned from Paul Boudreaux, who, mysteriously, had known quite a bit about her world.

"Why are you here?" she asked, breathless.

"Because I love you," Jack said. "I should have listened to you, even when the things you said made me think you had lost your mind. I should have trusted you because I loved you, just like I should have trusted Harper for the same reason."

She covered her mouth with her hand, trying to keep her tears at bay. God, she'd been so lost when he'd told her to leave. Lost and frightened and devastated beyond measure. She hadn't experienced such emotions since her parents had turned her over to the fairies. She'd gone back to the house long enough to leave Harper a note and then she'd run away, unsure about where she was going, but certain that she had to leave.

"How did you get here?"

"Boudreaux told me," Jack explained. "Said his family has lived in the bayou long enough to know about the portal between the two worlds. He told me that if I wanted you back, I had to wait until the waxing moon and damn it, Ana, it was the longest five days of my life. I crossed over the minute darkness fell and I've been searching all night for you, trying not to think that Boudreaux's moonshine was causing an epic hallucination. But now I've found you and I'm begging you to come back with me."

He dropped to his knees.

"I can't come back with you, Jack. I didn't make Harper's wish come true!"

"Yes, you did."

And as he explained all that had happened since she left, Tatiana fell to her knees, too, her legs no longer able to support her weight, and her wings, she noticed, now long gone. His crossing over, coupled with the truth of her success with Harper, had freed her at last. She threw her arms around him and kissed him again. As if she weighed no more than an enchanted feather, he lifted her into his arms and whooped as if he'd just scored one of those touchdown things he'd told her about.

Prince Ruprecht pushed through the tapestry and fumbled for his sword until he realized that his fairy godmother—*former* fairy godmother—was not in danger.

Tatiana laughed. "You were eavesdropping?"

"I'm a die-hard romantic," he replied.

Tatiana, utterly confused, decided that Ruprecht's problems were no longer hers. She wished the prince luck in finding a princess, then snuggled into Jack's arms as the giant stole her out of the castle and carried her all the way to the forest, through the smoky barrier and back up to his tall house in the bayou.

Fog had settled on the clearing that surrounded the house, making it look like a castle in the clouds. Tatiana might have believed that this was all a dream, but the sensations and emotions coursing through her were incredibly real. Jack didn't put her down until they reached his bedroom. He left her alone long enough to ensure that Harper was still asleep, probably dreaming of costumes and orchestras and audiences. Then he returned, stripped himself out of his clothes, and took very little time removing hers.

They stood across from each other, naked and bare, as the breaking sun flooded light through the windows. High on the top floor with the pink sky on the horizon, steamy mist below and the man she loved holding out his hands to beckon her to bed, Tatiana could hardly breathe.

"This is like a fairy tale," she said.

Jack laughed, lifted her one more time into his arms and carried her to the bed. This time, when he set her down, he pressed gently on top of her, torturing her every nerve ending.

"I don't know much about fairy tales," he admitted. "But I do know that I love you. You've given me everything I ever wanted, even though I didn't know I wanted it. Someone to share parenting duties with. Someone to share my bed with. Someone to share my heart with."

She shifted beneath him just enough to elicit his groan of pleasure. "Wish-granting *was* my job for a very long time."

His dark gaze brimmed with desire. "But now it's my turn to bring your fantasies to life, Ana. Tell me what you want."

"I want you, Jack. Right here, right now."

Jack might never have been sold in servitude to the fairies, but when it came to fulfilling her request, his special brand of magic made every single one of Tatiana's wishes come true.

# ONCE UPON A MATTRESS
## Leslie Kelly

To Julie...one of the bravest people I know.
Working with you has always been
one of my favorite parts of this job.

# *Prologue*

*ONCE UPON A TIME*, in a land not so far away as you might imagine, there lived a rather persnickety prince who refused to choose a bride. Though all the fairest princesses in the land were presented to him, the prince simply couldn't find one to meet his most exacting standards. Nor could he ever fully explain why none of them were to his taste.

So one day his mother, the powerful queen, took matters into her own hands. Determined to see her son married to a proper princess, she hired an expert tracker to go out into the world, find a suitable young lady and bring her back to the castle to be married to the prince immediately.

But you know what they say…you should never send a wolf to watch over the flock.

And the queen did, indeed, send a wolf.

# 1

ON ANY *other* night when the moon waxed on its inexorable journey toward full, Lucas Wolf would be outside, roaming lush valleys, fierce and untamed like his ancestors. As he ran free beneath the midnight sky, the moon's white-gold glow would bathe him in warmth and visceral pleasure. Every animal instinct clawed into his genetic code would fill with primal need to give himself over to his wildest impulses. And he'd do it, wholeheartedly.

That was, on any *other* night.

Tonight, Lucas was trapped inside a hot throne room, ready to howl with frustration. Instead of reveling in the warm glow of moonlight, he was pierced by the heated stare of a raging queen. And the only thing he might bathe in were the flecks of spit flying out of her mouth during her rant.

"Unacceptable, that's what it is. Simply unacceptable!"

"Mother, please…"

"Shut *up*, Ruprecht!" Queen Verona thrust a long, sharp-nailed finger toward her adult son. "If you'd been less picky, none of us would be in this situation."

This situation? As far as Lucas knew, the only one in a situation was Prince Ruprecht, who was known as the Charming—if not very bright.

A single man himself, Lucas didn't blame the prince for wanting to stay that way. Then again, lawmen like Lucas Wolf had the luxury of remaining single. At least until he found his one true mate—if such a person existed.

Lucas liked women. But never had he seen one he simply

couldn't do without…and he'd been keeping his eyes open for her. Until he found her, he was reserving judgment about his clan's one-perfect-mate-for-life concept.

Princes like Ruprecht did not have the luxury of waiting. Not as far as his mother was concerned, anyway.

"I'm not picky," the prince said with a sigh that verged on petulant. "I just haven't met the right person yet." He draped himself across his mother's throne.

"You've rejected every princess in all of Elatyria."

"Not quite," Ruprecht protested. "You were the one who sent that chit from the northlands away before I set eyes on her."

The queen's scowl deepened, highlighting the lines gouged into her forehead. For someone once called "the fairest of them all", she looked as appealing as a crone. "She was no princess."

"How do you know?"

"Her hair was lank, her skin pocked and she smelled of cabbage."

"I like cabbage." Amusement danced in the prince's eyes as he egged his mother on. "You didn't even put her to the test."

Princess tests? How bloody archaic.

"I wish I had! Because even a false princess-bride would be better than none at all. How many times have I told you, Ruprecht?" The queen crossed the throne room and put her heavily beringed hands on either side of the prince's face. "You must wed if we're to keep our grip on Riverdale."

Ahh. Lucas began to understand. Riverdale, a tiny kingdom to the west, boasted some of the richest lands in all the world. Queen Verona and her husband had taken control of it many years ago, absorbing it into their kingdom when the last surviving member of Riverdale's own royal family had died. Why, he wondered, would the queen be worrying about losing it now?

The prince rolled his eyes. "Who cares about stupid old Riverdale?" Charming he might be, but he was also spoiled and self-indulgent, Lucas thought. Not to mention lacking in common sense if he could so easily discount such a vital part of his future kingdom.

How like a petty prince to sneer at good land. For all commoners, fertile fields provided nourishment and security. But for those like Lucas, it was even more important. His own kind would be miserable trapped within thick castles built of stone. They much preferred simple sod houses. Some managed to run tiny wood-walled shops in the towns. But at heart, what the Wolf clan most longed for was land. Streams flush with trout, fields to cultivate when the moon was hiding, woods in which to hunt when it was full.

Lucas Wolf might be a lawman. He might track down evildoers and bring them to justice here in Elatyria or even in the other world that bordered his own—the one natives there called Earth. He might even be only one-quarter Wolf. But deep down, he understood why his father and brothers wanted a homestead of their own. He knew why they craved the chance to escape the towns and villages and live in peace in the country. In the wild.

Of course, that was next to impossible nowadays. The queen kept her sticky fingers wrapped around as much property as she could grab.

"I don't see why you're getting so upset about this, Mummy."

Mummy? This was the future king? *Terrifying.*

Queen Verona had obviously tired of her son's attitude. She smacked him in the head, sending his crown tumbling. "Marrying and providing the country with an heir is the only way to keep the people of Riverdale from demanding that the throne go back to the Mayfair family."

Ruprecht grabbed his crown and thrust it back on his head, realizing, at last, that his mother was truly worried. His brow scrunched in confusion. "I thought the line had died out."

The queen cast a quick glance toward Lucas, then admitted, "Not exactly. There is one heir left. The daughter of the late Queen Lenore. The queen's consort was a commoner from…over *there.*"

Ahh.

"So where is she?" asked Ruprecht.

"Shortly after her mother died, the young Princess Penelope fell from a turret and was badly injured." She tsked. "I hear she lost so much blood they thought she was already dead when they found her."

The queen didn't sound particularly sympathetic.

"Her father decided he wanted to raise her over *there*. Better medicine or something." She shrugged in disinterest. "In any case, Ruprecht, he asked your late father—whom he had befriended—to look after Riverdale, with the understanding that the girl would return on her twenty-first birthday to take her rightful place."

Curious, Lucas asked, "When is her twenty-first birthday?"

The queen shifted her gaze. "It was a few years ago. The child didn't return. I doubt she ever will."

"Then why do we have to worry about it?" Ruprecht asked.

The queen's face appeared harder than the statues of her that, by law, stood in every town square. "Because she *might*. Solidifying our hold on Riverdale is your responsibility. You must give the people a prince to claim and fawn over. Winning their hearts will ensure they aren't swayed by the Mayfair name, should the princess ever come back."

It made sense, Lucas supposed. He had grown up a day's ride from Riverdale, and he'd never heard stories of a long-lost princess. So he didn't imagine the locals were pining for her return.

Or had Queen Verona let the rumor get out that the girl had died? He wouldn't put it past her.

"You've made a fine mess of things," the queen continued. "No heir. No wife. No girl in all the lands good enough for you." Queen Verona wrung her hands together and stalked around the room again. "What are we to do? There's not one single princess left that you haven't refused or insulted. Not one."

The rumors about the prince's pickiness? Now those Lucas *had* heard. Ruprecht had reportedly told the exquisite, sung-about Princess Aurelia of the Glades that he would sooner kiss one of the frogs from the castle moat than touch his lips to hers.

Huh. Sounded as though the prince had been reading some of his own family history.

Queen Verona finally stopped her pacing and stood directly in front of Lucas. "This is why I brought you here. They say you've never failed to complete a mission. Is that true?"

"It's true."

"Good. I want you to scour the kingdoms and find out if there are any princesses my brilliant son hasn't mortally offended. Perhaps we can cajole one into reconsidering his suit."

Royalty. They intermarried too much and it obviously did a little brain-draining with every subsequent generation. Because there was another answer. It was so obvious, Lucas couldn't help rolling his eyes, surprised that she hadn't seen it.

"Are you looking to leave your head behind when you depart, lawman?" the queen asked, her face growing as red as the rubies that studded her crown.

Lucas continued to lean indolently against a column made of the finest dwarf-mined marble. He wasn't one of her subjects and didn't give a damn for royal manners. He'd come here because he'd been told she had a well-paying job for him.

Money was all that mattered these days. He'd achieved his quest for vengeance over the death of his little sister, an innocent who'd seen something she shouldn't have and had paid with her life. Having caught the last of the men responsible, it was now time for Lucas to get back to some kind of normalcy.

Only one force drove him these days, and it required a lot of coin. He wanted land. Wanted it for his father. His people.

"Well? Speak up or I'll have you skinned."

He sneered. The royal family didn't rule any Wolf.

"There is another answer," he said, trying to force a note of respect into his voice, though he felt none for the vain woman. But she had deep pockets and his were unfortunately shallow.

Queen Verona simply stared, waiting.

"The prince has to marry a princess, and there are none

who will have him. And you must solidify your hold on Riverdale."

"Yes, yes?"

How on Elatyria did these people manage to find their way across the castle without someone drawing them a map?

"It's obvious," he explained. "You simply have to send someone out to find Princess Penelope, bring her back here, and marry her to Prince Ruprecht."

"DON'T LOOK NOW, Princess, but that sexy, dangerous-looking drink of water in the corner is eyeing you like you're a rare burger and he's a reluctant vegetarian dying for some meat."

Penny Mayfair cringed as her friend and boss, Callie, used the nickname her late father had given her as a kid. *Princess.*

Pretending she hadn't heard, she loaded two ham-and-egg specials and a dozen side orders onto a serving tray. Idly hoping the cook hadn't left any eggshells in this order, she turned away from the heated, pass-through window of the diner's kitchen.

"He didn't want me to wait on him," added Callie, who owned this place. Having been Penny's late father's girlfriend for many years, Callie was the closest thing Penny had ever had to a mother. The woman, a romantic at heart, was never happier than when she was matchmaking. "Asked for you twice!"

Penny frowned, glancing across the packed diner. Every table was full and she was doing double duty today. Gina, the other full-time waitress at Kallie's Kuntry Kitchen, had called in sick. As usual. Gina was a wild child who always hooked up with a guy named Jack Daniel's or his buddy Johnny Walker on Saturday nights. So she was never in the mood to serve Jimmy Dean on a subsequent Sunday morning.

Callie was an angel, but her arthritis made waitressing a real chore for her. Meanwhile, Glen, the cook, was in a rotten mood because somebody had sent back a too-runny omelet, so he was intentionally ass-dragging on every order.

Not the type of day when Penny Mayfair felt like dealing with demanding customers.

"He's at table eighteen."

"Can't he see I'm busy?" she said with a weary sigh.

Not waiting for an answer, Penny snaked her way to table twelve. She slung the plates full of food at the two oilfield rough-necks who'd ordered enough breakfast for a family of five.

"Thank ya, *Princess.*"

"Shut up, Eddie."

"Aww, that any way to talk to your best tipper?"

"Here's a clue for you," she said with an amused eye-roll. "Leaving me a note on a napkin saying, 'Here's a tip, bet on horse number two,' doesn't earn you a lot of points."

Eddie, a good-natured good-old-boy who parked himself at the same table every time he came in, snorted and slapped a hand on his knee. He and many of the other guys who worked out at the oilfields came into LeBeaux a couple of weekends a month, looking for the closest town that boasted a bar.

LeBeaux had three. Which was two more than the number of banks and one more than the number of restaurants.

On Saturday nights, guys like these tried to hook up with girls like Gina. On Sunday mornings, bleary-eyed and obnoxious, they showed up here.

"I got a tip for ya, baby," said Eddie's dining companion. "Say yes and you won't regret it."

He grinned, but good humor didn't light up in his eyes the way it did Eddie's. This guy was a stranger. His reddened nose and bloodshot eyes, plus the reek of whiskey that surrounded him like Pigpen's cloud, told her he was a hard partier. She'd been on her guard the minute he'd sat down.

"So, what time do you…*get off?*"

Oh, great. Like she hadn't heard sleazy come-ons like that a million times since she'd turned sixteen and started slinging hash at this place. Considering the lack of women in the area, it was almost expected. Penny rolled her eyes and turned to attend to the next table.

Then she felt a hand on her butt.

*Son of a....* She whirled around and jabbed an index finger in his face. "The next time you put a finger on me, you're gonna have to start pulling off your shoes to count to ten."

"Oooh, feisty! I like it."

Eddie frowned at his friend. "Hey, no need for that, Frank."

"Oh, miss? My coffee?"

Glaring at the perv, Penny hurried over to grab the coffee-pot. Seeing the way her hand shook, she fought to stay cool.

What was it with men who thought they had the right to manhandle any woman they wanted to? And why her? Everything about her—from her aloof demeanor to her short hair, her multiple piercings, her clothes and her tattoos—screamed that she wasn't a bimbo looking for action. So why did everyone want to give it to her?

According to Callie, it was because no matter what she did to herself, Penny could never hide the fact that she was beautiful. And beneath her gruff surface, she was sweet-natured and vulnerable.

Penny told her that was bullshit. Even if, deep down, she feared Callie was right.

Wouldn't everyone in town have a laugh if they ever figured out that tough little Penny Mayfair, was, at heart, an orphan looking for a home.

She sighed, not willing to go there today. Not when it was only two weeks until her twenty-fourth birthday. Meaning it was almost three years since the day her father had died, leaving her by herself in this huge, lonely world.

Penny thrust the image of his kind face out of her mind and got back to work. Turning her attention back to the orders getting colder under the heat lamps and the people waiting to check out, she hurried to wait on the next table.

But then she stopped. All thought stopped. Time itself even seemed to stop. The clatter of forks on stoneware and the cacophony of raised voices faded into one soft background hum.

Penny's rubber-soled high-tops stuck on the cracked linoleum and she stumbled a step, then came to a standstill. Her heart paused mid-beat. Maybe the rest of the world did as well.

Because there he sat. The tall drink of water at table eighteen who would have to be gulped because a sip would never be enough.

*Lord have mercy.*

It wasn't the man's size that stunned her, though the way he towered over the table said he was incredibly tall. And though the bench seat was built for two, no way could anybody else sit on it with him, not with the breadth of those shoulders.

It wasn't the blunt attractiveness of the stark, masculine face, with the slashing cheekbones and strong brow. Or the jutting, grizzled jaw—not bearded, yet his five o'clock shadow was going on midnight despite the earliness of the hour.

It wasn't the thick, nearly jet-black shaggy hair that brushed across the leather-jacket clad-shoulders.

It wasn't the powerful hands curled together on the table. Or the curve of the sensual lips. Or the aura of danger that seemed to roll off the man like heat off a bonfire.

No. It was his eyes that got to her, leaving Penny speechless and confused. Dark, nearly-black eyes were focused entirely upon her, staring with utter concentration. They looked almost feral. But she didn't feel threatened. In fact, for some strange reason, the word that popped into her mind when she noticed the way he watched her was *claimed*.

It was a strange feeling, considering she had no one in this world who had a legitimate claim on her. She should know, she'd looked. She was totally without family. There was absolutely nobody who could, or would, ever call her theirs.

Until him. The guy eating her alive with his stare, who looked like he expected her to accede to any demand he cared to make.

*Nobody makes demands of me.* Requests? Okay. But not demands.

She finally began to breathe again, to think again. But she couldn't prevent a final, quick mental acknowledgement that she had never in her life experienced anything as jolting as this man's possessive stare.

She slowly stepped closer until she stood by his table, staring down into the fathomless depths of those inky eyes.

He murmured, "And here you are."

Deep voice. Rough. Throaty. It scraped across her nerve endings and made her skin prickle. "What?"

He shook his head, as if he hadn't intended to speak. "Tell me you're not the one they call Penny Mayfair," he ordered.

Swallowing, she admitted, "Sorry. That is my name."

His furrowed brow said he wasn't pleased by the news. His muttered curse confirmed it.

"What do you want?" she asked, forcing away all those crazy, gushy sensations that had awakened and begun to do somersaults across her most girly parts at the sight of him. Hearing his voice had turned those somersaults into gigantic loop-the-loops.

*No loop-the-looping with strangers. Got it?*

Hooking up with a guy she picked up in the diner would simply confirm peoples' opinion that she was pure white trash. Besides, if there was one thing her wild, cross-country quest to find *any* member of her family had taught her, it was that the answers to her questions weren't going to be found in the arms of some hot stranger.

"This can't be happening, not now, not *you*," he muttered, staring at her hard, his dark eyes gleaming with something that verged on need.

*Wishful thinking.*

He spoke again, under his breath. "You *can't* be the one."

Her annoyance rising, she snapped, "The one what?"

He looked away, and she saw the way his pulse was pounding in his temple, as if he were undergoing some great internal struggle. Finally, he said, "You *really* are the princess?"

Her eyes narrowed. "Shut up."

She had to get Callie to lay off the nickname. Her father had gotten away with it throughout her younger years, even though she had never played princess, seen a Disney movie or owned a frilly doll. She couldn't recall ever believing in a happily-ever-after, or even reading a fairy tale in her childhood. So the princess thing had been her Dad's little inside joke.

But now that he was gone, the nickname needed to go, too. She was about as far from a pink-tulle-and-diamond-wearing-princess as she was from a green-skinned alien chick on some old sci-fi show.

"Princess?"

"Call me that again and you'll be wearing breakfast rather than eating it." Her words lacked any heat. Penny was simply used to resorting to snark when anybody started to hassle her.

His eyes gleamed though his stern expression didn't waver. "But you haven't served me any food with which to break my fast."

She jerked her thumb over her shoulder toward the closest table, even while noticing the odd way the man spoke. "There's plenty of food over there."

"Consider me warned."

He slid out of the booth and rose to his feet, forcing her to tilt her head back to continue meeting those eyes.

*God, he's tall. Huge. Freaking gorgeous!*

As if knowing he'd sent her thoughts spinning, he stepped even closer, until their bodies almost touched. His was massive, strong, rippled with muscle. Hers, soft, curvy and yielding. A perfect fit. Her mind suddenly flooded with images of all the lovely ways they could fit together.

"No," she insisted, more to herself than him. "This is crazy."

"I know," he admitted. "It's still happening."

"*What* is?"

"I've been looking for the princess. And I've been looking for *you*. I just never expected they'd turn out to be the same person."

Totally not following, Penny could only stare.

He didn't explain, just watched her, his gaze hungry. "I'll fill you in later."

She quivered, her ears tricking her for a second into

thinking he'd said he'd *fill* her later. Because, oh, God, did she suspect he could.

His lips widened in a knowing smile, as if he knew exactly what she'd been thinking. "Later," he repeated. "Now, back to my mission. Your full name is Penelope Eloisa Mayfair?"

Damn, she hated that name and did everything she could to keep people from hearing it. How this dude could have learned it was beyond her, but right now, she didn't care. She just wanted to keep him from repeating it. "Would you lower your voice?"

A lot of people in this town already looked at her as though she was a two-headed freak and her eccentric name wouldn't help. Sure, she might have lived among them since she'd been a child, but to most of them, she'd always been an outsider.

She hadn't fit in. Not ever. Those who didn't consider her arrogant and snooty because of how well she did in school looked down on her for not being interested in any of the things that fascinated the other local girls.

"I need to confirm your identity," said the stranger.

"It's confirmed, okay? Now what do you want?" She edged closer, trying to hide him from nearby diners. Pointless, really. It was like a mouse trying to stop anyone from seeing the grizzly bear in the corner. "In case you haven't noticed, we're busy and I'm stressed."

"Why not quit?"

She couldn't help laughing. "I have bills to pay. Ever heard of not wanting to starve?" Then she glanced around at the awful food cooked by Glen-the-talentless. "Okay, I guess you have. Avoiding starvation is probably the only reason anyone would come to this place." She kept her voice low, not wanting to offend the regular clientele, or Callie. No point making herself stand out even more.

Penny's differentness had been made even more obvious a few months ago, when she'd come back after going on a two-year-long journey to find out who she was and where she belonged. The trip that had confirmed that whole you-have-nobody hypothesis.

She'd hit the road shortly before her twenty-second birthday, with one goal in mind: discovering her own past. Dad, as much as she loved him, had been keeping secrets all her life. Secrets about his own background and definitely about Penny's mother's. He'd promised to give Penny answers when she grew up.

Unfortunately, he had died before he could keep his promise.

So Penny had set off on a quest, following the few clues she had. They'd led to nothing but more questions. Eventually losing hope, she had kept wandering, trying to find someplace that resonated with her soul. She'd gone from city to city, town to town. In each, she'd tried out a new job, a new hair color, a piercing, a tattoo, or a man before moving on to the next.

And she'd discovered she didn't really fit in *anywhere*. No one location was better than the last. Each left her feeling…restless. Out of step, out of touch. Adrift.

In that old movie, Dorothy had said there's no place like home. For Penny, no place *was* home.

So she'd given up. Decided that having her hopes raised and then crushed was worse than just not knowing. Penny had come back to her father's old house, her few friends, and to Callie, the one remaining constant in her life. She'd dragged all the remnants of her journey along with her. They were stamped on her body, on her mind and on her spirit, proof of her efforts to identify the real Penny Mayfair.

Oh, hadn't that given the residents of LeBeaux something to talk about! Despite being lovingly welcomed back by a few, to the town's old guard, she'd simply proved what they'd always suspected of her—that she was bad news.

"Are you all right?" the stranger said. He spoke softly, knowing she could hear, as if they were so in tune to each other that the symphony of gossiping voices and slinging crockery didn't exist.

"I'm fine."

Penny shook off her sad thoughts. Things were okay, *she* was okay. Not fabulous. But okay. She had a job, she had a roof over her head and she had a few true friends, which was better than having dozens of phony ones. She managed to maintain her wild-child image that kept people from looking closer and seeing anything she didn't want them to. And she sometimes even had fun doing it.

*This is not a bad life.*

Even if deep in her heart she knew it wasn't the one she had been destined to live.

"What is it you want?" she asked.

"I want you to come with me."

A shiver of excitement danced through her, even as she formed an instinctive refusal. "I'm not going anywhere with you."

"Yes, you are." As if realizing he couldn't exactly force her out through the packed restaurant, though he seemed tempted, he grudgingly added, "I must speak with you."

People had begun to notice their confrontation. They were all eyes, all ears, dying to be scandalized by the town's bad girl.

Penny sighed. "I don't have time for this."

"It's urgent."

"Yeah, right. If you lay that 'Come with me if you want to live' line on me, I'm going to stab you in the eye with a fork."

Though, that might be tough. The guy was staring down from what had to be a good foot advantage, and she was no shorty.

He merely shook his head, continuing that intense, searching perusal of her face, her hair, her black-clad form.

"You're *truly* Penelope Mayfair? Daughter of Lenore Mayfair?"

She gasped. "What the hell do you know about my mother?" Penny had no memory of the woman who'd given birth to her. She'd never even seen a single photograph, since her father had said they'd all been lost during a move. So for this stranger to casually throw out the name stung sharply.

He shook his head, apparently unfazed by her sudden anger. His expression suddenly appeared almost regretful as he asked, "You weren't a foundling, I assume? No chance you were adopted?"

Penny's hand fisted. Whatever this crazy attraction was about, it couldn't overcome her instinctive need to protect her privacy. "Get out."

"How old are you?"

"I'm twenty-four." *In two weeks.* She had replied before even thinking about it. Why she was answering this stranger's questions, she had no idea. But that was it, no more.

"Where is your father? Did he abandon you?"

This time, Penny didn't listen to the voice of caution that said he was a big, scary-looking dude who knew too much about her. She stomped on his booted foot. Which just served to hurt her rubber-covered arch and didn't so much as make him flinch.

"Why did you do that?" he asked, tilting his head in visible confusion and not a bit of discomfort.

Penny ignored the pain in her foot and glared at the man. "Because you're seriously pissing me off. Now go away."

"Sorry," he said, shaking his head and looking anything but repentant. "You're not going to get rid of me that easily."

"Easily? I think I broke a bone in my foot."

He shrugged. "Not my fault."

Glaring, Penny considered stomping on his foot again. Or punching him. But as if he read her thoughts, he narrowed his eyes in warning. "Don't even think about it. That shot was free. Next time, I defend myself."

"Oh, am I supposed to be all scared now?" she snapped, probably sounding more brave than she actually felt. "You think you're tough enough to intimidate me?"

Okay, that was dumb, because he was pretty damned intimidating. Though, honestly, she didn't truly believe he would hurt her. Not only because they were surrounded by people in a public place, but because something about him seemed more 'big, overbearing protector' than 'bad guy'.

Penny had always had good instincts about people. Those

instincts told her that while this man was going to annoy her in ways she hadn't yet begun to comprehend, he wouldn't hurt her. The same instincts had warned her that the roughneck, Frank, was a nasty character. And he'd proved that with one disgusting grope.

This stranger was different. Not that he couldn't be trouble, but she didn't experience that instant shiver of awareness that said he was someone you wouldn't want to turn your back on for fear of getting a knife between your ribs or a hand on your ass.

She could handle him. Really.

Though she felt a moment's panic when he inched closer, keeping his voice low as he finally answered both of her questions.

"You should definitely be scared. Because if you swing at me one more time, Princess, you're going to find out exactly how intimidating I can be."

# 2

—————

IT WAS FUNNY. Lucas had thought *finding* Princess Penelope would be the hard part when, in fact, it had been remarkably easy. Queen Verona had told him where the girl's father had said he was taking her, and to his surprise, she'd still been here. He had picked up her trail right after he'd arrived this morning.

But he suspected locating her would be the only easy thing about this job. Getting her to come with him would be a problem.

Figuring out how to *keep* her was going to be an even bigger one.

But keep her he would. Because there was no way he was going to let her go. Not when, from the moment he'd laid eyes on Penny Mayfair, he'd wanted her with every ounce of his being.

It had finally happened. He'd looked on a woman and known he'd sooner cut off a limb than do without her.

And she was the princess he'd been hired to deliver to another man's marriage bed.

"Oh, miss? My coffee?"

Lucas glanced past Penny at an impatient-sounding man sitting at a nearby table. Leveling one slow, steady stare at the stranger, he noted that the man swallowed and pushed his empty coffee cup away, reaching for a glass of water instead.

"Look, you're making a scene."

"You're the one who kicked me," he rebuked, amused by her temper. It brought out the fire in her beautiful eyes.

"I didn't kick you," she snapped. "I stomped on your foot."

"So come with me to make amends."

Finally, as if too frustrated to argue, Penny said, "Fine. Meet me outside in five minutes. Got it?" Apparently seeing his hesitation, she added, "I'll be there. I promise."

He watched her whirl away, wondering if she would keep her word. But he had no other choice. Short of dragging her out by force, there was nothing he could do but go outside and wait.

It was just as well. The air was better. Not good, but better than inside the cramped, reeking diner.

Lucas didn't like to spend too much time on the Earth side of the world. It was too loud, too frenetic. Much too crowded with people jammed together in their cities, driving their screeching automobiles, moving much too fast. All his highly attuned senses went into overdrive whenever he crossed the border.

There were times, when doing his job, that he'd had to cross into areas far worse than this. The city of New Orleans was a torturous maze of noise, colors and odors. Like all his kind, he had a keenly developed sense of smell. So the scents, in particular, were so overwhelming he felt incapable of breathing.

While in New Orleans, he'd experienced its darkest side. He had gone into dingy, rundown hotels, had staked out seedy tourist traps. He'd followed suspects into vampire-themed bars where the other patrons had no idea the creatures of their imaginations actually existed in other realms.

At first glance, the Mayfair princess seemed more suited to one of those places than to this small country dining hall. From the purplish tinge in her short, spiked black hair, to the heavily made-up skin and darkly shadowed eyes, she looked like anything but a member of a royal family. Except, perhaps, for Snow White...*after* she'd been in that glass coffin for a while.

But those eyes. Those dazzling, purple-violet eyes proclaimed her lineage. From what the stories said, they were a trademark of the Mayfair women.

Then there was the face. Her lips were full, her chin a bit stubborn, her cheeks soft. Finely boned, delicate and almost fragile, Princess Penelope's face would, without a doubt, be utterly beautiful when washed clean of the layer of cosmetics and about a decade's worth of mistrust.

But the rest. Great Rumpel's ghost, she was nothing like he'd expected. Nothing like anyone had expected.

Spoiled, petted princesses often wore jewels. But not, as he recalled, hoops of silver dangling from the lobes of their ears, with smaller rings and studs riding all the way up each curve.

Her black clothes looked more appropriate for a crone than for a young woman on either side of the border. The only relief from the solid black came from the garish, bright-red canvas shoes that extended all the way up over her ankles.

The top and loose skirt hung baggily over her body, concealing much of her shape. But from where he'd been sitting, by the door, he'd gotten a few glimpses of her calves and thighs outlined beneath the filmy fabric. The tight, black leggings she wore beneath the skirt clung to those limbs, highlighting the slenderness, the length.

He'd seen her maneuver through the crowded room with platters of food, serving others, waiting on those far beneath her in stature. He'd heard her snap at anyone who tested her and watched her manage ten tasks at once.

He'd also seen her defend herself against an oaf who had laid hands on her without permission. That was fortunate, for Lucas had been rising from his seat, his hands clenching into fists the moment the stranger's shifty eyes had hinted at his dark thoughts. A low, black cloud of anger had overtaken Lucas's vision and he'd almost launched himself across the diner when the bastard had dared to touch her.

But she'd taken care of herself.

Something told him she always took care of herself.

She was also someone who could be taken at her word. Penny proved as much by showing up at the door exactly five minutes after he'd exited. She burst outside. "Okay. You've got my attention. Tell me what you want, and then go away."

Lucas crossed his arms over his chest, leaned against the

door to make sure she didn't dart around him to go in, and nobody else could come out. Then he answered. "I am indeed going away. Far, far away. And so are you."

Her mouth opened, then closed. For the first time since he'd seen her, she was entirely speechless. He sensed it didn't happen often. This was a woman who was seldom lost for words.

She was tough. Ragged. Hard-edged. Outrageously dressed, pierced and made-up. The idea of her presiding over the genteel court of Riverdale was ludicrous. Queen Verona would *never* accept this woman as the bride for her spoiled Prince Ruprecht.

Which, actually, was a good thing. Because there was no way Lucas could deliver Penny Mayfair into another man's hands.

Not when he was determined to make her his own.

"OKAY, let me get this straight," Penny said after the stranger had finished his ridiculous explanation. "You say you represent my mother's people? And that you have to take me back to her homeland to claim some old inheritance?"

The big, sexy man, whose glorious eyes appeared to have a hint of gold in them out here in the sunlight, nodded, unaffected by her obvious disbelief. "Exactly."

Though her heart fluttered, Penny quickly stifled her excitement. Because things like this just didn't happen to her. Life was *never* this easy, not in the real world. She hadn't gone on a fruitless, two-year journey of exploration only to have some hot dude in a black leather jacket show up out of the blue to provide answers to all her questions.

"But you won't tell me where you want to take me or what this inheritance is? Or even who, exactly, sent you to find me."

"Correct."

"And you think I'm going to say, 'Okey-dokey,' grab my stuff and blindly follow you to the ass end of nowhere."

He cast a long glance at her, visually assessing her admittedly unusual clothes. For some reason, one corner of the sensual mouth pulled up a bit in what was probably his impersonation of a smile. "You don't need to pack much. You should definitely come as you *really* are."

He said it as if he didn't mind her wardrobe, which Callie called her Witch-of-the-West look, completed by the ruby-red high-tops.

"You're missing the point. The issue isn't my packing."

"It isn't? What other issue is there?"

Oh, maybe just the little one that this total stranger thought she would instantly trust him and let him whisk her away to who-knew-where to do who-knew-what.

Well, okay, some of the who-knew-what might be good. But only if *she* decided she wanted that 'what'.

"The issue is, you can't show up here and expect me to follow you like a dumb sheep."

Though following him would entail walking behind the man. And considering the way his faded jeans hugged those incredible thighs and lean hips, she honestly wouldn't mind getting a look from—and *at*—the rear.

"I'm no shepherd," he said, something gleaming in the depths of those eyes.

"More like the big bad wolf," she muttered.

For some reason, he suddenly coughed, lifting his fist to his mouth as he turned his head to the side. Finally, after he'd cleared his throat, he said, "We don't have much time, Princess. We have to go now."

There he went with that stupid nickname again. She blew out a huffy breath, then curved her hand around one ear, tilting her head to the side. "What's that? I think I hear something. Oh, yeah, it's the nuthouse calling. They want you to bring back their straitjacket."

He merely lifted a brow. The man seemed incapable of being provoked, as if, despite his dangerous looks, he really knew how to hold onto his temper. "What can I say to convince you?"

She hesitated, wanting to walk away, yet tempted—so damn tempted—to listen to what he had to say.

Part of her was dying to know more about who sent him.

Her mother's *people?* Meaning, people who'd actually known her mother, whom Penny couldn't even remember? People who might be able to fill in the blanks of her history—tell her why Penny had been able to find no record of her mother's existence, not *anywhere*. Maybe explain why there was no proof of her parents' marriage. No record of where her father had lived for a good ten years of his younger life. Why her own birth certificate hadn't been filed until Penny had been three years old.

So many questions. No answers.

*Until now?*

Finally, taking a chance, she said, "All right. Here's how you convince me. Tell me everything. Every single detail. Let me hear it and then I'll decide if you're crazy…or I'm *crazier* and actually believe you."

He frowned. Instead of making him look forbidding, it just added to the whole super-hot-bad-boy thing he had going on.

"I can't do that."

Stabbed with disappointment, she immediately reached around him for the door handle. "Yeah, that's what I thought you'd say."

He refused to get out of the way. "You wouldn't understand, not right now."

"Look, Mr.…what is your name, anyway?"

"It's Lucas Wolf."

An appropriately tough one. Then she rolled her eyes. No wonder he'd reacted when she'd called him the big bad wolf. What was it, the name for words that sounded like what they were? Onomatopoeia? Yeah. That fit. His name definitely fit his whole big, bad self.

Besides, she'd bet he *was* a wolf as far as females were concerned. He sure had the looks for it, if not the flirtatious charm. Not that he probably needed to rely on charm or seduction. He was all tough, overpowering, alpha man who women flocked to like…well, like sheep.

Women often chose to settle down with nice guys. That

didn't mean they didn't have fantasies about one last, wild fling with a dangerous, edgy man who was relentless in his pursuit. Many such females would probably have said, "When do we leave?" after hearing his proposition.

*But not you.*

No. Not her. Parts of her anatomy might already be packing her bags to follow him anywhere. But above the shoulders, she was firmly grounded in reality. She'd sown her wild oats. Big-time.

She'd also followed far too many promising trails that led only to disappointment. She was done with all that. No more expectations meant no more disappointments.

"Well, Mr. Wolf, you're wasting your time. If you won't give me any more information, then our conversation is finished. I need to get back to work."

"Tell me you don't want to come with me, that you're not dying of curiosity."

She hesitated, then finally lied. "I'm not."

In truth, this tall, sexy stranger probably couldn't have said anything that would have enticed her more. Still, the fact that he *was* a stranger—a dangerous-looking one—meant she couldn't consider going along with what he was asking. Aside from not wanting to set herself up for yet another disappointment, her instincts about people could be wrong this time. For all she knew, he could be the son of the Son of Sam.

"Hello?" a muffled voice said. Someone knocked on the glass door behind Lucas, obviously wanting to exit.

"You should let those people out. And I have to go back in."

"No."

He put a hand on her arm, and everything…*changed.*

Sizzling heat and pure electric energy erupted at the spot where hand met arm. More, though, there was a strange sense of recognition. As if confirming that she knew him far better than she should after such a brief acquaintance.

There'd been interest from the very start. This was something different. Something *much* bigger.

Penny sucked in a slow, uneven breath, astounded by the rush of pleasure that came with the unexpected contact. Her loose, gauzy shirt was thin enough to feel the indentation of each strong finger, though he didn't clench them. It didn't hurt in any way, yet she felt almost branded by the fire of his touch.

*Claimed.*

As crazy as it sounded, she felt as if she was finally discovering who she really was, where she belonged. Just the pressure of his grasp, that hint of restrained power, affected her like no other touch she could remember.

It was disconcerting, unnerving. Good, but also too surprising to deal with on the spot.

Somehow, she managed to keep still, merely staring at him until he silently unhanded her, the reluctant gentleman inside winning out over the overpowering male.

Well, maybe not a gentleman. But a decent guy.

*Stop it, you don't* know *that. You can't be sure!*

Even after he'd let her go, their eyes remained locked, and confusion flashed briefly in his. As if he, too, had been taken by surprise by an instant rush of feelings.

"My apologies." He stepped aside to let the customers out.

Penny frowned. His speech was so strange. He was rough-looking, but could also be polite, almost old-fashioned. He used normal words, yet once in a while something sounded off.

A family eased out, casting curious stares at Penny and the stranger before heading up the block. The second they were out of earshot, he put his hand on her again, clasping her shoulder with determination.

So much for thinking he'd decided to be a gentleman. She shivered, though whether it was because she was glad or worried, she honestly couldn't say. "Didn't you apologize for grabbing me?"

"No. I was apologizing for accosting you in front of the door where people could see."

"And now what, it's accost away?" Her words lacked anger. She didn't feel a bit accosted. Just warm and tingly again.

"I have you alone and I need you to agree to come with me."

She cast a pointed stare toward the windows. Lucas turned, blocking her view…and blocking her *from* view of those within.

"Say you'll come."

"And if I say no, are you gonna tie me up and toss me into a big bag, tough guy?"

His response flew out of his mouth so quickly, she didn't believe he planned it. "If I were to tie you up, Princess, I wouldn't be tossing you anywhere but flat onto your back."

Whoa. Penny swallowed hard, hearing the frustration in his voice, that note of bare, thin restraint. The cords of muscle in his neck flexed and he was breathing hard through obviously clenched teeth. Everything about him screamed at some supreme effort to remain in control.

She knew what he was trying to control. Oh, did she ever.

The man wanted her, and he'd been trying to keep himself from doing anything about it. When he'd touched her, he hadn't been surprised by his reaction, but by the fact that *she* felt the same way.

Before, there had been attraction. Now there was pure hunger.

The claiming she'd sensed earlier hadn't been about making demands *of* her…but of demanding *her.*

She knew that given half a chance, he would take her wildly. Passionately. He wanted to back her into the alley between the diner and the shop next door, yank her clothes out of the way and plunge into her, right up against the side of the building.

Or that's what she wanted. Whatever.

It was instantaneous. Primal. Completely instinctive.

"Who *are* you?" she whispered.

Frowning, as if he didn't like this thing that had sprung up between them, he said, "The man you've been waiting for."

The man she'd been waiting for. *Forever?*

Her body reacted both to his visible lust and her own mental response. Even as Lucas dropped his hand again, as if already regretting being so blunt, Penny's nipples tightened and swelled with need. They were super sensitive anyway, and now, at the thought of those big hands touching her and that hot mouth tasting her, all her nerve endings practically sat up and begged. She wanted to rip her own shirt off, to tweak and stroke, to gain some relief.

He noticed, his hot stare zoning in on the swell of her breasts. No way could he not see how he affected her. The want in those eyes made it seem for a second as though he could peer all the way through her clothes.

"Princess," he groaned, low, cautionary. It was as if he was begging her to stop tormenting him.

Huh. *Him?* She was the one who was suddenly being betrayed by her body. The one whose feminine impulses, so long dormant, had awakened with a vengeance.

She had to clench her thighs together to keep them from trembling and to try to contain the swelling of her rapidly moistening sex. That only served to tighten the pressure around her clit, which already throbbed with need.

Funny that she hadn't even thought about sex in months. Now she suspected she wasn't going to be able to *stop* thinking about it until she'd had it—with this man—at least a dozen times.

Her heart began to thud, her skin to prickle with anticipation. Each breath she drew was filled with his scent—earth and musk and sweat and man.

Lucas closed his eyes, visibly trying to regain his calm. He seemed deeply affected by the subtle changes in her body, each hidden sign of feminine desire. His deep breaths and the faint flare of his nostrils made her wonder if he could actually catch the aroma of arousal that seemed to permeate her every pore.

He shuddered slightly, licking his lips. As if he could taste her on the air. Which simply inflamed her all the more.

*Are you insane?* They were standing outside the diner, in broad daylight. Even if the people inside couldn't see her, anybody walking up the street certainly could.

This crazy interlude—which was like having sex without

a single intimate touch—needed to stop. Now. And she knew how to stop it. Sheer bravado had gotten her out of many tough scrapes.

"So, uh, do you have a thing for tying girls up, hotshot? Does that make you feel strong?" she finally asked, intentionally baiting him. Her tone wasn't suggestive and there was no purr of invitation that said she wanted him to subdue her. *Even though you do.* She was all gruff, bitchy attitude, albeit her voice was a tiny bit weak and breathy.

"Only those who need to be," he growled. "And the thought of having you held in place, forced to lie back and be pleasured, doesn't make me strong, it makes me weak in the knees."

Oh, shit. Talk about out of the frying pan. Her own knees knocked together and she wobbled, needing to stick a hand out to steady herself. That hand landed on a big, broad chest.

"Stop it," she whispered. "This is crazy."

"Trust me," he urged.

"Trust you? I don't even know you."

"Yes. You do," he insisted. "Deep down, you know you do. Give me a chance. Come with me."

She swallowed as he stepped closer. So close his boot slipped between her feet, his jean-covered leg sliding temptingly between her thighs. Hot and hard and so overwhelmingly male it was all she could do not to sink down and straddle him, ride him, use him to gain some much-needed release.

Gazing at the hint of skin revealed by the white shirt beneath his jacket, Penny's mouth went dry. It had been a long time since she'd run her lips along a ridge of hard muscle or tasted salt-tinged male flesh.

That flesh was darkly tanned, the neck powerful with cords of muscle that met solid-granite shoulders. A hint of curly dark hair on his chest made her wonder how low it went, if it narrowed to a thin line down a flat, rippled stomach before disappearing into the waistband of his jeans.

"Please."

For a second, she wasn't sure if he'd whispered that word or she had.

Shaking her head hard, she forced her thoughts back where they needed to go. On the safe and normal present. Not on any wild, crazy adventures with Mr. Shagalicious Hotness.

"I can't listen to this any longer. It's crazy in there."

*Crazier out here.*

He hesitated, glanced over his shoulder toward the restaurant full of angry, impatient customers. Sighing heavily, he narrowed his eyes and stepped away. "All right. We'll talk after you're finished work."

She let out an unamused laugh. "I'm not going to be out of here until 10:00 p.m., at the earliest."

His jaw, which looked even swarthier than it had twenty minutes ago inside, clenched. "Ten o'clock? At night?"

"That's generally what 10:00 p.m. means." Realizing she might have sounded as though she was asking him to wait for her, she quickly clarified, "That wasn't an invitation to come in and wait."

"I don't intend to."

So much for convincing her. Penny couldn't help wondering why the abrupt comment stung a little. "Whatever," she said, stepping around him and tugging the door open.

He cleared his throat before she could step inside. "Nights are…" He looked up into the sky and rubbed a hand against his jaw. A big, strong hand. That stubborn, hard jaw. "…not good."

Funny. She sensed a night with this man could be *very* good.

*No. No thinking that way.* "I can't do this. Not here. Not now. Please let me go," she said.

"We don't have much time, Penny."

It was the first time he'd called her by her real name. Oh, it sounded nice from those lips. And a bit of her resolve melted.

But when she heard the clatter of crashing dishware, that resolve reformed and hardened. Inside, Callie stared helplessly at the floor. She'd dropped a tray filled with empty plates, probably unable to bear the weight.

"Damn," Penny whispered, stabbed with guilt. "That's it, we're done." Then without offering Lucas Wolf one last moment to try to change her mind, she strode inside and got back to work, determined to forget about the dark, mysterious man.

# 3

THIS WAS *definitely* going to be harder than he had expected.

Princess Penelope didn't trust him. Considering Lucas had skimped on the details to make them somewhat more believable, he imagined she would run away screaming if he admitted where he *really* wanted to take her. Who she really was, who her mother had been. The whole, "There's another world that everybody over here thinks is fiction, but really does exist," issue.

She would have laughed in his face…even though she wanted him. Badly. Oh, he'd noticed. Her obvious lust for him had nearly driven him out of his mind.

He had never been so close to letting his primal urges wash over his human common sense than in those charged moments outside the diner. She couldn't have been more inviting if she'd torn off her clothes and begged him to take her. Over. And over.

Heaven help him, he'd wanted to. Over. And over.

But even the hint of desire he'd shown had made things worse.

"You should have stayed all business," he told himself as he rode on his Harley early that evening, having just turned around to head back to LeBeaux. He'd been cruising for hours, staying away from towns, not wanting to be around people. But the sky would soon darken. Even if his eyes hadn't sensed the difference in the quality of the light through his sunglasses, he'd have known the sun would soon set. He could feel it in his blood. Feel the tug of the moon wanting to take over the sky.

If he were smart, he'd stay out until morning, not risk

trying to appear normal. Because, when the moon was full, *his* normal was a little different from that of the people on either side of the border. Nothing drastic, not like the stories of ravaging predators. But he couldn't deny that he looked, acted and felt a bit strange at certain times of the month.

It could be worse. He wasn't, after all, a full-blooded member of the Wolf clan, since his mother had been a human from over here. Most other Wolves had far more noticeable traits.

Feeling a hum against his hip, he remembered the cellular phone he used when visiting these lands. He kept it with the Harley, clothes, money and false identification in a small abandoned shack near the border. Only one person knew the cell phone number.

He pulled over onto the shoulder, thrust a booted heel against the kickstand and cut the engine. Pulling the phone out of his pocket, he answered, not surprised when he heard his half-brother's voice.

"So you *are* here."

"How did you know?"

Hunter, to whom Lucas's mother had given birth after she'd left Lucas and his father to return to her own world, laughed softly. "I always call when the moon's full on the chance you crossed over while you could."

"Why?"

"Well, *you* might have a dozen half-brothers over on your side of the divide, but you are all *I've* got."

"Don't you have a mate now?" Lucas chuckled, knowing how to get under his brother's skin. "A very attractive one as I recall."

"Don't think I'll ever forget that you've seen her naked."

"Oh, I won't let you forget, I promise you," Lucas replied, well remembering the day he'd climbed into bed with a sleeping woman who'd thought he was his brother.

At the time, Hunter had been tracking him, trying to capture Lucas for crimes he'd thought he had committed. Capturing the woman had seemed the simplest way to get his brother to stop trying to kill him long enough to listen to the truth.

"If and when the day comes that you settle down, I might have to pay you back. Unless you end up with a real…dog."

Hunter snickered, and Lucas rolled his eyes. "With such wit, you should be on that box for fools that everyone over here seems to be in love with. I can see you fitting in with the people on one of those, what are they called, reality shows?"

"One TV show about a bounty hunter is all the world needs."

"I was thinking of the one where people with no singing ability perform in front of ridiculing judges. You're a natural."

"F. U."

Lucas glanced at the sky. "I need to go."

"Are you anywhere nearby? Want to meet up for a beer?"

Startled, since his relationship with Hunter had always been more of a long-distance one, both physically and emotionally, he replied, "Sorry. Nowhere near New Orleans."

"Too bad. Scarlett would like to get to know you. One of these days, you need to stick around between full moons. I'd like to see you, but I'd prefer not to do it at that time of the month when you're, you know, PMSing."

"What's PM—" He heard his brother laugh. "Never mind."

After finishing the call, he again checked the western sky, noting the sun had dropped further toward the horizon. He was hours from LeBeaux. Riding under the stars with the powerful engine between his legs and the wind whipping through his hair was one of his favorite things to do over here.

*So ride all night. Go back to see her in the morning.*

The idea had merit, and probably made sense. Given his mood, not to mention his instantaneous reaction to her, he should steer clear until sunrise. All those dark, hungry urges he'd been so unsuccessful in hiding from her this morning would be more powerful tonight.

But an inner instinct wouldn't let him stay away. He didn't know why, but he had the sense that something was wrong. Maybe even dangerous. And Lucas trusted his sixth sense, he always had. He felt compelled to go back to that dusty, dour little town. Back to *her.* Not tomorrow. Tonight.

He set off again, mentally deciding on a plan. He'd lay low, near her house, keeping an eye out for whatever danger he sensed was coming. Then he'd approach her first thing in the morning.

He had one more day to convince her. After that, the border crossing would be too thick to traverse. He'd have to go home, wait until the next full moon approached, then come back and try again. No way would he consider spending a full month over here.

Queen Verona, however, wasn't the patient type. And while he had no intention of allowing Penny to marry that idiot Ruprecht, he still intended to fulfill the contract by bringing her back to her homeland. But he didn't entirely trust Verona not to renege on the deal if she had a month to think about it.

No, he couldn't wait a month. He simply had to convince the princess to come with him.

*Or just take her.*

If he did that, however, he couldn't guarantee they'd end up at the castle. Because taking her by force was one step from claiming her altogether. His deepest impulses already screamed for him to carry her to his cabin, lock them both inside and have her until she acknowledged what he already knew.

That she was his. Penny Mayfair, that beautiful, wild-haired, wild child, was the woman he wanted.

He still couldn't quite believe it, even though he'd always been told it would happen. That someday, he would meet a female he couldn't do without. Like others of his kind, he would know her and would do anything to have her.

It had nothing to do with love. It was simply the way he and those like him were made. Some believed every body contained only half a soul, that mates were simply the soul's recognition of their other halves. Lucas had no idea whether that was true. He only knew he'd seen her, and he'd wanted her. Forever.

It was that simple.

There were a few sticky problems, however. He would be escorting her back to the homeland to be inspected for marriage. Oh, he knew Queen Verona would not allow Penny to wed her precious son. Lucas could deliver her, wait for the five minutes it took for the queen to faint in horror, then escort Penny out of the castle. Having completed the job he was hired to do, he would collect his payment—both gold and deed to some land the queen had offered to sweeten the deal—on his way out the door.

Afterward? Anything. First, he'd take her on a trip throughout the land she'd been denied since childhood. Something told him she was going to like that world. Perhaps it was the rebelliousness she exhibited here, where she *thought* she was supposed to be, that told him she was unhappy. Or maybe it was simply a recognition of someone who, like him, was never entirely sure where she belonged. Part of one world, part of another.

*She might not stay.*

His mother hadn't been able to stand being away from her old life. She'd chosen it over her Wolf husband. And Lucas.

But Penny was different. She had been born over there. Elatyria was her home. Her birthright.

*What if she decides to claim the* rest *of her birthright?*

It was possible. She might decide to pursue her throne. The idea that a Wolf could end up with the Queen of Riverdale was almost as ridiculous as seeing Penny in the arms of that weak-kneed Ruprecht. But he'd deal with that when it happened.

The churning thoughts filled the trip back to LeBeaux, and by the time Lucas reached Penny's hometown, darkness had fully descended. Each hour had brought the full moon—that enormous full moon—higher in the sky. The night wasn't entirely clear and the white-gold orb was occasionally blocked by swathes of misty clouds as long and silky as great sheets of black cloth. Whenever its light was extinguished, he felt the loss on every inch of his skin, each strand of his hair, right down to his core.

Just as everything else was bigger over here, including time itself, the moon seemed double its usual size. It consumed half the heavens, quietly powerful and mysterious, a silent answer to his own body's cry for recognition.

Maybe this world wasn't *all* bad.

Though he knew the princess's address, instead of heading to her house, which he'd located this morning, he swung by the diner. Smart move, as it turned out. A quick glance confirmed she was closing the empty restaurant for the night.

"Long day, your majesty?" he murmured, watching from up the block as she and an older woman stood chatting outside. They were both softly silhouetted beneath a streetlight on the corner.

All the other shops around them were closed and dark. That wasn't surprising, given the hour. This area of town boasted mostly small, dusty businesses and a few residences. The two people in front of the diner were the only ones in sight.

But they weren't alone. Oh, no. A predator was in the vicinity.

Lucas wasn't referring to himself.

He tensed, his heart pounding within his chest. Though his breaths remained even, they deepened, filling his lungs as if in preparation for some fierce exertion. Beneath his taut skin, his muscles tightened and flexed, instinctively readying for conflict. His fingers clenched tightly around the handlebars of his Harley, until the thick pads dug into his palms. He released them and curled his hands into two tight fists.

*Why? What is it? What's wrong?*

He remained still, so still. His acute hearing picked up the soft murmur of the women's voices. He heard nothing else.

It didn't matter. He sensed the presence. Hell, maybe he just *smelled* something dark, ugly and malevolent.

He slowly stepped off the bike, moving silently into the shadow of a nearby shop. He walked lightly, not wanting even the sound of the heels of his boots hitting the sidewalk to betray his proximity. Then, tucked safely out of sight, he froze, remaining motionless. Waiting.

Their conversation carried to his hypersensitive ears.

"Goodnight, Penny. Thanks again for working a double shift. Sorry you couldn't run off with that sexy guy this morning."

"Run off?" Penny said with a grunt. "You have no idea."

"Well, if you get the chance again, you *go* for it," the other woman said, reaching out and touching Penny with what appeared to be a tender hand. "I know you haven't been happy since you came back here. As much as I love having you around, please don't feel like you need to stay because of me."

"Here's as good as anywhere," Penny replied, sounding wistful, resigned. Which merely cemented what he already suspected about her feelings for her homeland.

*You don't belong.*

"Besides, *you're* here." Though it didn't seem like something that came naturally to her, Penny put her arms around the other woman's shoulders and hugged. She just as quickly stepped back. "And you need me. Who else is going to haul your butt out of the fire when Gina calls in sick?"

"She's going to have to grow up one of these days."

The princess smiled. She looked younger now, softer in the darkness without the sun spotlighting the thick, unnatural makeup. "Keep dreaming."

The women exchanged goodnights, then separated, heading in different directions. As she walked, Penny rubbed the back of her neck with one slim hand. The slump in her shoulders and the trudge of her feet told him she was exhausted. Not paying close enough attention to her surroundings.

Obviously she didn't notice *him,* though he felt sure his heated stare must be burning her from a block away.

Knowing the danger was directed at Penny, not at her coworker, who'd walked off the other way, Lucas followed the princess. He remained on the opposite side of the street, hugging the buildings and the shadows and the silence. At one with the night.

As she left the puddle of light from the streetlamp behind her, Penny was completely swallowed by darkness. The next streetlight wasn't working.

*Coincidence?* Possible. But he doubted it.

The full moon played a game of hide-and-seek with the thick clouds that had followed him steadily from the west, so even it wasn't able to provide much illumination. Yet he saw her, heard the soft scrape of her rubber-soled shoes on the sidewalk. If he stood still and concentrated all his attention on it, he thought he might even be able to hear the beating of her heart.

He also smelled the light, flowery scent—feminine, and at odds with her tough-girl appearance—wafting from her skin. Just as he'd smelled the wanton need arising from her this morning.

She lived a few streets away and apparently assumed this town was a safe one. She seemed fearless as she walked home, alone, late at night, without a care in the world beyond the pain in her tired feet and aching arms.

*You're not safe.* The words screamed in his head yet didn't emerge from his vocal cords.

A second later, he was proved right. He spotted a movement in the shadows ahead of her. Five, seven paces, no more.

The danger. The presence he'd sensed stalking her waited directly in Penny's path.

Lucas didn't think, didn't shout, didn't do anything except run, silent, furious, afraid for her. His feet nearly flew over the street even as rage clouded his vision and grabbed him in its blind, ruthless grip.

But he didn't make it. Even at his fastest, he still wasn't quick enough to stop Penny from being grabbed and violently hurled to the ground.

IT HAD BEEN one long, miserable day. Nonstop customers and nonstop drama had led to a nonstop headache. By the time ten o'clock had rolled around, Penny had wanted nothing more than a steamy-hot shower and an icy-cold beer, both of which awaited her at her small house a few blocks away.

The attack came out of nowhere. She had been oblivious to any threat. Entirely comfortable back here in LeBeaux, she hadn't foreseen the dangers she would have routinely guarded against in New York or Chicago. She had simply meandered into the path of trouble. And between one step and the next, she found it.

"No," she cried as a dark shape hurtled from between two buildings, launching itself at her. Her assailant tackled her to the ground. She cried out as her shoulder hit the cement hard and his big form hit her even harder, covering her, pinning her.

He grabbed a fistful of her short hair and twisted, slamming her head down. Pain rocketed through her, but she didn't waste any breath trying to scream. Instead, she reacted instinctively. Operating purely on adrenaline, she fought back as if her life depended on it.

*Which it might.*

"Let me go!" Penny curved her fingers into talons and tried to rake her attacker's face, which she couldn't make out in the darkness. Drawing her knee up as quickly as she could, she aimed for his groin, knowing she'd hit home when he grunted in pain.

"Bitch," he said in a hoarse whisper, obviously trying to disguise his voice. But it didn't matter. The reek of booze and the rank smell of his breath told her immediately who had attacked her. It was Frank, the grabby oilfield roughneck who'd come in with Eddie this morning. He obviously hadn't gone back out into the field, instead lurking here, lying in wait to finish what he'd started this morning.

"Let me go." She tried to wriggle away, hoping she'd hurt him enough to gain a few seconds head start, but his fingers clenched painfully around her arms.

"You're not going anywhere."

"No, but *you* are," someone else snarled. Frank was lifted off her with abrupt, brute force. "You're a dead man!"

Penny rolled out of the way, looking up in time to catch a glimpse of a familiar profile.

*Lucas Wolf.* The stranger who had so affected her this morning had come to her rescue, grabbing her attacker by the throat. He shook the man, holding onto the front of a flannel shirt and slamming his fist into the bastard's face. Frank had been caught by surprise, but quickly regained himself. He tried to fight back, swinging wildly, something glittering in his hand.

"Watch out, I think he has a knife," she called.

Another blow from Lucas's fist and the glittering thing went flying to shatter against the ground. *Broken glass.*

A car exited a nearby alley, briefly illuminating the scene in its harsh headlights. Just a flash, then it was gone, speeding away.

But that quick glimpse was enough to stop Penny's heart. Given what she saw in that flash of headlights, she had to remind herself to breathe, not believing what her eyes were telling her.

It had to have been a reflection of the car's hazard lights that made Lucas's eyes glow red. Or else she'd taken a harder blow to the head than she'd thought.

But there was one thing she wasn't imagining. Lucas's long, thick hair hung down around his face, which was grizzled and dark with a new-grown beard. And his lips were pulled back in a grimace, revealing sharp, white teeth as he audibly growled at the man with whom he fought. His expression defined fury.

The encounter was over within another minute. Despite landing a punch on Lucas's face, Frank soon realized he was far outmatched, dealing with an opponent who looked driven by pure bloodlust. After a blow sent Frank spinning several feet, he took advantage of the distance and took off at a dead run.

Lucas took a step, hunched forward, his powerful body leaning as if he planned to run the other man down like a hunter after fleeing prey. Then he hesitated and looked back at her.

Penny was still on the ground. A little dazed, a lot stunned.

And she'd probably have one hell of a headache tomorrow. Not from the blow to the head, but because she intended to go home and have a few shots of tequila to wipe out the crazy thoughts that had been going through her mind for the past few minutes.

Thoughts about those reddish eyes and that snarl on his face. The way Lucas Wolf had looked almost feral. The long, wild hair. But the strangest thought of all? That she wasn't afraid. Not for herself, anyway.

Lucas's rage seemed to ease as he let the stranger go and hunched down beside her. "Are you all right?" he asked, his tone gruff, yet laced with concern.

Penny simply stared.

"Princess?"

"Jeez, would you lay off the Princess stuff? Call me Penny, okay?" Realizing she sounded like a flaming bitch, not exactly the appropriate reaction to someone who'd probably saved her from a serious assault, she closed her eyes and shook her head. "I'm sorry. I'm a little shaken up."

He didn't give her a moment's warning before he scooped her up into his arms, rising to his feet and cradling her against his chest. He acted as though she weighed no more than a baby.

"Hey, what are you…"

"The hospital or your house?"

She stared up at that rugged face, but couldn't see him well in the darkness. She wanted to glimpse the gold in those brown eyes, and a ghost of a smile on his sensual mouth. But the eyes shone black in the night and his mouth was compressed and hard. Despite the care he was taking of her, anger still enveloped the man.

"Penny? Do you need me to take you to the hospital?"

Finally realizing he was waiting for her to make a decision, she shook her head once.

"What about your head?"

"It's okay," she mumbled, lifting a hand to touch the small lump already rising behind her ear. Her fingers came away flecked with a small amount of moisture. *Blood. Oh God.*

Her head started to spin. She hated the sight of blood. Hated the smell of it. The feel of it. Hated anything to do with it. It was her one weakness.

And suddenly, like some vapid heroine in an old movie, her eyes drifted closed and she felt herself sag heavier in his arms. She came within a breath of fainting, but somehow, when he clutched her even tighter and she felt the strong, steady, reassuring beat of his heart, she didn't do it.

"Hospital," he snapped.

"No, it's fine," she insisted. "I'm not badly hurt. Just a little stunned." The fact that she hadn't eaten a thing today didn't help.

Nor did the thought that she'd seen this man's eyes glowing red a few minutes ago.

She swallowed. "The truth is, I get really woozy at the sight of blood."

"Then you'd better close your eyes again," he muttered.

But he didn't say it soon enough. The moon peeked out from behind a cloud, and she suddenly got a better look at the man holding her so carefully in his massive arms. At the abrasions on one cheek. At the trail of blood dripping freely from the cheekbone down, likely nicked by broken glass.

This time, there was no stopping it. Darkness clouded her vision and that sense of dizziness she'd been fighting washed over her completely. It took away thought and fear and reason.

And consciousness.

# 4

ONE OF THE FIRST things he was going to do once Princess Penelope regained consciousness was lecture her about her security. Even with her in his arms, his single kick had busted the flimsy lock on her front door. Prowling around the house—after he'd lain her on her bed—he'd found the window in the bathroom unlocked. Not that her window locks were of much use, anyway.

She didn't have a single weapon, as far as he could tell. If she had to defend herself, the best she could do was to grab one of the dusty, unused frying pans from the kitchen.

"Do you have *any* sense of self-preservation?" he asked her still form.

Lucas glanced toward the bed, then back into her bathroom mirror as he scraped a flimsy plastic razor over his cheek. It wouldn't do for long, given the full moon, but he didn't want to scare the woman to death the minute she opened her eyes and noticed that his beard had grown a couple of inches from this morning. A half inch of that since he'd rescued her.

Adrenaline, the chase, the fight…they sped things up.

"If he had been smarter, the bastard could have been here, inside, waiting for you to get home."

The thought made that roiling surge of anger rise in him again, but he quickly shoved it away. He'd deal with the attacker later. Lucas had his scent. The man wouldn't be able to hide from Lucas's rage no matter which side of the border he was on.

"What?" she whispered.

"Finally." Dropping the razor, he approached the bed. As

he stared down at her, he noted the color in her cheeks. When he'd wet a cloth to clean her cut, he'd also taken a minute to wash all the makeup—not to mention dirt and gravel—off her face.

She was, as he'd expected, beyond beautiful.

He wondered if she even realized it. If the clothes, the makeup, the attitude, were all because she didn't care how she looked, or because she *did* care and didn't want anyone else to realize how striking she truly was.

He suspected the latter. She'd been hiding in plain sight.

She blinked a few times. "How long have I been out?"

"Minutes. Ten at most."

She shifted and slowly sat up, looking at him with frank disbelief. "And in ten minutes, you carried me three blocks home, broke into my house, put me to bed, then had time for a *shave?*"

He answered with a shrug. Because, yes, that's what had happened. Her slight weight hadn't slowed him down.

Penny continued to stare up at him. The confusion slowly left her face, and color entered it as her gaze grew more intimate. She parted her lips to breathe and the pulse in her throat, which he could see—and almost hear—fluttered.

God, the woman really needed to learn how to hide what she was thinking. Considering he was trying like hell to keep his own secrets, knowing how much she wanted him didn't help.

*Later. Want me later. When I don't have to be strong enough to resist you.* He had to be strong now. Not only because he still had a job to do—bringing her home—but because he couldn't take what the woman was offering until she understood exactly *who* she was offering it to.

She wasn't entirely happy about it either. Her small jaw stiffened, as if she needed to imbue herself with resolve. "I can't believe you used my razor."

He shrugged. "I'm not worried about using something that has come in contact with your legs." Far, far from it.

More of that color appeared, more of that confusion. More of that feisty attitude. "Yeah, well, how do you know my *legs* are all I use it on? Huh? Maybe I use it somewhere a whole lot more intimate than that."

He considered her words for a moment, then realized what she meant. This time, he was sure his face filled with color, so hot was the explosion that rocked through him. His heart was definitely beating harder, his breaths thick, each one tasting like *her*.

"That I'd like to see," he admitted before he could stop himself. He'd heard of women over here sporting that smooth, shorn look, but he'd never actually seen it himself. The trend might eventually make its way over to Elatyria—with the number of travelers back and forth between the lands on the rise, some other customs were certainly making their way across.

Frankly, he could have done without *ever* seeing a gnome with a one-inch ear gauge.

She sputtered, rising from the bed. "I was kidding."

Shoving away a flash of disappointment, he insisted, "You don't have to get up to defend yourself from me. I wasn't about to rip your clothes off to see if you were telling the truth."

Those lavender eyes hadn't darkened with fright; she didn't fear him. Which was good, she didn't need to. Although how she could know that, he couldn't say. He wondered if she felt it too, the instant connection. The certainty that they were supposed to be together. It went beyond mere wanting. Though, right now, mere wanting was pretty powerful in and of itself.

"I'm sorry, I'm being a shrew. You bring out the beast in me for some reason."

*Mutual.*

"You saved me from something pretty awful tonight."

He frowned at the thought. "He won't get away with it."

"I know. I'll contact the sheriff in the morning. But I doubt he's anywhere near here. He probably won't stop running until he hits the Gulf of Mexico."

"He can run as far as he wants to," he muttered.

"Anyway, thank you, Lucas. For saving me, for bringing me

back here, taking care of me." She moved closer, the soft smell of her perfume filling every molecule of air between them.

"You're welcome," he replied, his voice just as low.

He didn't know what she intended. At least, not until she rose on tiptoe and leaned toward his face. Saying nothing, she brushed her soft lips across his in a touch as fleeting as a caress from a summer breeze.

Lucas gritted his teeth and steeled his will. Fisting his hands by his sides, he used every ounce of his power to remain still, not grab her in his arms and kiss her with all the deep hunger he'd felt for her since the moment he'd seen her.

"Why did you do that?" he asked, his throat tight.

He expected to hear a stammering response—*It was a thank-you kiss, an expression of my gratitude.* Instead, he got pure honesty. Pure Penny.

"I wanted to."

Some deep-rooted masochistic gene made him growl, "Do you want to again?"

She nodded once. "Yeah. A *lot.*"

With a groan, Lucas gave up all resistance. The invisible restraints that had seemed to bind him erupted in an explosion of pure hunger. He wrapped one arm around her waist, cupping her chin in the other hand. Dragging her up, he bent to meet her, and their lips crashed together and parted.

As Penny's warm tongue thrust against his in deep, hungry tastes, he swallowed down the wild, untamed flavor of her. He tilted her head to one side, his to the other, needing to go deeper, wanting to devour her whole, from the inside out.

They kissed deeply, paused to gasp for air, kissed again. Penny pressed against him, her soft body molding against his. He couldn't stop himself from lowering his hand, brushing it down her neck.

"Oh, please, keep touching me," she whispered against his lips, arching up toward his fingers.

As if he could stop. Lucas slid his hand down, determined

to be careful, not to hurt her the way he knew he could, especially at this time of the month. When he wanted to be...wild.

Brushing the soft curve of one breast, he let his thumb slide down over its taut tip, which thrust provocatively against the filmy shirt.

She hissed when he reached his prize and plucked at it. "Oh, God, yes."

He kissed her deeply again, sucking her tongue into his mouth, imitating what he wanted to do to her nipple. And her sensitive clit, which he was dying to see, touch, taste.

She didn't have to beg him to give her what she wanted. He knew by her tiny whimpers, the cries in her throat. Without thought, without planning, he tugged the fabric up, lifting his mouth from hers just far enough to pull the shirt all the way off her. Then he touched her again, feeling warm, puckered flesh.

Plus something else.

"What the..." he muttered, looking at the beautiful breast in his hand. Perfectly formed, pert and lush. And *bejewelled*.

"What the hell have you done to yourself, woman?" he asked, somehow pushing the words out of a throat that felt too tight to keep bringing necessary air into his lungs. Because while part of him wanted to spank her for marring her perfect body so painfully, another part was sure he'd never seen anything as wickedly erotic in his life.

Two pretty silver rings hung from the tips of Penny Mayfair's breasts. The Princess of Riverdale had pierced her nipples. But from her rapturous cries as she thrust harder against his hand and ground her groin against him, pain was the *last* thing she was thinking about. Which meant she had done it for her own pleasure. She liked the sensations it wrought.

Her fingers twined in his long hair, tugging him down her body. Lucas could no more refuse than a starving beggar could turn his back on a feast. He pushed her back onto the bed, dropped to kneel between her legs, and buried his face in her bare stomach. Licking, biting lightly, he worked his way up, rubbing his cheek against the under-curve of one breast. He again ordered himself to be careful, to go slowly and not hurt her, even though a primal need urged him to be rough and hard. Fast and demanding.

He managed to keep himself under control, although he didn't know how. Nor could he say for how long he'd be able to, either.

"Please, do it!" she ordered, sounding frantic as she tugged at his hair and arched toward his mouth.

Patience was a virtue, but his was never strong when the moon was full. He groaned before moving his lips to one perfect tip, covering it, sucking hard, swirling his tongue around the pretty silver ring. He tasted warm metal and warmer, sweet skin.

"Yes," she said with a deep sigh.

While tasting one, he plucked the ring on the other breast with his fingers. She hissed when he increased the pressure, tightening her fingers in his hair to keep him where she wanted him, urging him to suck deeper, to tweak harder. Her legs twined around his waist, the core of her landing unerringly on the long ridge of his rock-hard cock. She instinctively thrust toward him.

Lucas groaned and thrust back, taunting them both. The musky, feminine smell of her overwhelmed his senses. He had to close his eyes and breathe her in, memorizing her scent, imprinting it on his brain and in every cell of his body.

"More. Give me more, Lucas."

He wanted to. God, did he want to. But as he opened his eyes and saw his own dark, swarthy hand against her pale skin, already reddened under his aggressive touch, something—some strong, deep instinct—made him stop. He couldn't take her until she knew. Couldn't claim her fully until she was aware of how much of herself she was giving.

*All* of herself. Forever.

With strength he didn't know he had, Lucas pulled back, thrust a frustrated hand through his hair, then rose to his feet. "I didn't come here to get some kind of payback." He staggered away, watching as she gasped for breath and slowly brought herself back under control. "You were unconscious not long ago."

It took a full minute, then, finally, her voice shaking, she said, "I'm sorry. I don't know what came over me." Not meeting his eyes, she grabbed her top and pulled it back on, covering that beautiful body.

Good. He didn't know if he could have kept up his resolve for another minute if she hadn't.

"I'm not the type to go around jumping on strangers."

"We're not strangers."

She didn't respond, not trying to argue. How could she? Something inside her had to be reaching out, responding to her heart's instinctive knowledge that he was part of her world—her *real* world, the one she'd been denied since childhood.

She'd recognized him, *known* him, at first sight, too. Now that she'd been in his arms, there could no longer be any doubt.

"You're hurt," he explained gruffly, seeing that she was shaken by his decision not to take what she had offered.

"I'm okay, really," she said, a forced smile appearing on her mouth as she tried to put things back on more normal footing. She was good at it, hiding her reactions, any hurt feelings. Queenly, in fact, in how easily she moved past the moment and brought the temperature back from blazing to merely burning. "A kiss of gratitude, that's all it was."

"Sure." *Uh-huh. Right.*

She flushed, then squared her shoulders and changed the subject. "So, is playing hero part of your job description?"

"I'm no hero. And you're not going to be as appreciative when you see that I kicked in your front door."

Surprisingly, she laughed. "There's a key under the mat."

"Are you *determined* to be attacked?"

"I can…"

"Take care of yourself. Yeah, I know."

She hesitated. "Except tonight. So thanks again," she said with a simple nod. Again, he caught a flash of her bloodline in the grace of the gesture, the way she held herself.

He admired that. But what he wanted was the wild woman who'd been writhing beneath him a few minutes ago. Not a princess, but a female in heat, at the mercy of her own hunger.

Lucas gritted his teeth, thrusting the images out of his head. Not only did he have a job to do, the woman had just been violently attacked. "Are you sure you're all right?" he finally managed to ask. "Your head, is it paining you?"

"A little, but I'll take a couple of ibuprofen."

Brushing past him to the bathroom, she opened a mirrored cabinet and removed a small bottle. Her gaze passed briefly over a blood-tinged washcloth and she swayed on her feet.

Lucas crossed the room in an instant and steadied her with a hand on the small of her back.

"God you're fast!"

"You're still dizzy."

"It really wasn't the bump that conked me out. I've had a major thing with blood for as long as I can remember. Just can't handle it—I tried to donate at a Red Cross blood drive once in high school and fainted in front of half the school."

She spilled two tablets from the bottle, popping them into her mouth. Then the wicked wench bent completely over the sink, spooning water between her lips.

Wanton images flooded his brain. Was she trying to kill him? That deep, mind-numbing kiss, the wicked eroticism of her body, her passionate response, now a provocative position designed to drive him wild? If not for the leggings she wore, it would be so easy to slide the skirt up, grab her hips, and thrust into her from behind until they both howled with pleasure.

She seemed oblivious, straightening and continuing with her conversation. "I guess I used to be pretty clumsy. My Dad told me I fell out of a window and almost killed myself when I was a toddler. I've had a problem with blood ever since."

*Focus.*

"Where is your father, Penny?" he asked, never having gotten an answer from her earlier today.

"He died almost three years ago." She waved toward the table beside the bed, on which stood a framed image of a younger Penny with a smiling, middle-aged man. "There's a picture."

"He died before you turned twenty-one?"

"A few days before."

"It all makes sense now."

One angry brow shot up. "Makes sense that my father died of a heart attack before he was even fifty years old?"

"No, no. I mean, it makes sense now that he didn't bring you to your mother's people. He wasn't alive to keep his promise."

"Don't go there again, please. Not right now."

"All right. But we have to talk about it."

Penny shoved a hand through her short hair, which had lost most of its jagged spikiness and fallen into short curls around her face. Everything about her, from her appearance to her mood, even the tone of her voice, had grown softer. More vulnerable.

"I miss him every day," she admitted, glancing again at the photograph.

"I'm sure you do."

He understood such grief. The loss of his sister had left a hole in him that he didn't think would ever be refilled.

Still introspective, Penny tilted her head, glancing toward a shelf on the wall above the bed. On it sat a sizeable box wrapped in pretty paper, with a large bow on the top. The paper was faded, the bow dusty. The gift had remained unopened for quite some time.

"From him?"

She nodded. "Callie, my Dad's girlfriend, gave it to me when I came back to town a few months ago. He'd had some stuff stored in her garage and she found it after I'd left to go…traveling. He must have stashed it there in case I went snooping around our place."

"Why didn't you open it?"

Her moist eyes tugged at his heart. "It hurt too much. Opening it seemed like the final step in admitting he's gone."

"I see."

She managed a weak smile. "Anyway, I turn twenty-four in two weeks. I figured I'd hold out until then. It'll be one last present from my dad on my actual birthday."

She deliberately turned her back on the shelf, the photograph, the sad thoughts. "Look, I owe you big-time. And I have decided you're not a serial killer, because you could have taken me out while I was unconscious a few minutes ago."

"Thanks. I'd hate to think you go around inviting serial killers to kiss your pretty nipples."

Color rose in her cheeks. "The point is, I will let you spill whatever it is you came here to say to me. But it's late, and I've had a long day. Right now, all I can think about is taking a hot shower and eating food that doesn't include gravy, breading or old grease."

Though his stomach rumbled at the reminder that he had not had a meal since he left home, her words made him grateful he hadn't ordered anything at the diner. "You have eaten nothing all day?"

"I serve that food, I don't actually consume it."

Nodding, he gestured toward her shower, squelching the image of her standing inside it, naked, steamy streams of water gushing over her beautiful body—making those little silver hoops glisten and shimmer. "Take your shower and I'll make us a meal."

"Us?" One delicate brow arched over her eye. "You're inviting yourself to dinner?"

"It's the least you can do," he pointed out.

A small frown appeared, but she made no saucy comeback. Nor did she order him to leave. Nodding once, she said, "Deal. There's tons of produce in the fridge. I am dying for a salad."

He grimaced. Lucas was dying for a big, so-rare-it-was-almost-mooing steak.

"I'll be done in a few minutes, okay?"

"Fine."

*Or lamb chops. Mmm.*

She probably saw a quick flash of hunger on his face.

Though, he'd been trying to hide such a look since the moment he'd laid eyes on her, so it shouldn't have showed. "Just make enough for both of us. I'm starving."

"I don't do salad."

"Big bad wolf must have meat, huh?"

He let out a surprised bark of laughter, unable to help it. Damn, the woman had no idea what she was into here. Had no clue that being this close to her, especially now, with the fullness of the moon right outside, was filling his head with strange, dark, frenzied fantasies. Hunger. More intense than his need for food.

He didn't want to hurt her, wouldn't harm a hair on her head. He just wanted to devour her in the most sexual way possible.

He couldn't stay here much longer. In fact, he should have left already, hidden nearby to watch over her for the rest of the night. That coward who'd accosted her probably wasn't fool enough to stick around, but there was no telling.

But he didn't want to leave yet. Her spirit was coming back, she was returning to her normal, feisty self. He wanted more time with her. "Actually," he finally replied, "I could go for a steak. A very rare one."

She wrinkled her nose. "Well, good luck with that. Because every store around here is closed." She put her hands on his chest and pushed him out of her bedroom with a smirk. Just before closing the door in his face, she added, "And I'm a vegetarian."

## 5

"GOOD GRIEF, he must have a beard made out of steel wool!"

Wrapped in a towel, Penny stared down at her bare legs, which were flecked with pieces of tissue. The flecks had once been snow-white, but were now turning red as blood soaked through. She steeled herself against the queasiness and looked away. *Tiny flecks, that's all. You've nicked your legs before.*

But not usually a dozen times at once.

She had been out of replacement blades for the razor. Since she'd only used the blade once before today, however, and hadn't figured Lucas Wolf's sexy face could do too much damage to it, she'd included a quick shave with her shower.

Bad move. She looked as though she'd lost a fight with a vengeful kindergartener armed with a sharp stick.

She should have ignored the feminine vanity and skipped the process. It wasn't like he was going to get close to her calves or thighs, anyway. He'd had his shot and hadn't taken it.

*Maybe he will if you don't take no for an answer this time!*

She ignored the salacious inner voice that had sounded like Angie, a tattoo artist she'd met and befriended in Detroit. The woman had talked Penny into doing some crazy things.

"Forget it, he turned you down," she reminded herself as she went into her room to grab some clothes. And she couldn't take another rejection. Not when she wanted him so badly.

Thinking about it, though, she realized he hadn't looked happy about stopping. In fact, he'd acted like someone had started pulling his fingernails out. So maybe he was being the gentleman who she suspected lurked within that big, sexy body.

Penny donned a Metallica T-shirt and another loose, elastic-waist skirt that wouldn't brush up against the nicks. Giving her head a shake, she ran her fingers through her wet hair—one definite advantage of such a short do.

As she left her bedroom, she cast a quick glance toward the wrapped box on the shelf and was stabbed with the same mix of emotions she always felt when she looked at it. Amusement, grief, happiness, regret, love. Such love. Then she left her bedroom.

True to his word, Lucas had begun preparing them a late-night dinner. She entered the kitchen and found him frowning down at the stove, where something sizzled in a frying pan she hadn't used once in the past nine months.

Yuck. "I said I didn't want any fried…." Her voice trailed off and she came to a sudden stop as he looked over at her.

She'd been in the shower maybe fifteen minutes. Twenty tops. And yet he looked *so* different. "You must have more testosterone than an entire major league football team!"

"What are you talking about?"

"I massacred my legs with the razor you used, and here you are, looking like you need to use it again."

He glanced away. "Did you use it anyplace else?"

Wicked man. Trying to change the subject. As if he couldn't have found out for himself a little while ago, anyway. She'd been so turned on he could have stripped her naked and done her out in the street and she wouldn't have objected.

Damn the man for starting something and not finishing it.

*You started it.*

Well, there was that.

"Perhaps the blade was dull to begin with," he added. "That must be why it wasn't effective for either of us."

Funny, she seemed to recall lying on the bed, looking up at him during their previous conversation about where she'd used the razor. And thinking how nice those smooth cheeks might feel on the inside of her thighs if he made good on his threat to tear off her clothes and see for himself.

Then, when she'd kissed him, touched his face, felt him scrape his cheek against her incredibly sensitive nipple, there'd been the tiniest hint of roughness, but that was all.

She shivered. Because now, those cheeks weren't smooth. And while she couldn't deny that the rough stubble would probably feel even better against her uber-sensitive skin, she just wanted to know why.

"Veggie burgers," he muttered, staring at the pan in disgust. "Whoever created them ought to be put in the stockade."

That didn't distract her. Penny had been busy and distracted this morning. Injured and woozy, and eventually horny, tonight.

Now she was clear-headed. Fully cognizant that something about this man didn't make sense.

It wasn't just the beard. She also wanted to know why his speech sometimes sounded so odd. Why he insisted on taking her with him somewhere, refusing to name the place. Why he had been following her tonight. What the hell the reddish eyes and the sharp-toothed growling had been all about.

And, damn it, why had he stopped when everything from his eyes to his mouth to his hands to that big ridge against the seam of his jeans said he was dying to screw her brains out?

Penny had never read fairy tales as a kid, but that didn't mean she had no imagination. While she might not believe in unicorns or fairies, she was open to other possibilities. Her good instincts had told her on occasion that she was meeting someone…different. Out of place.

Once, at around age eight, she'd come home early and found her father talking to a strange-looking man, small of stature, long of face. She had immediately felt that he didn't belong here. Not just in Louisiana, but *anywhere* she'd ever known.

There had been other occasions. Only a few, but each time, her inner voice told her she was meeting an outsider walking a lonely path where he did not, *could* not, ever fit in.

She saw that now in Lucas Wolf. Maybe she'd seen it from the start, but her attraction had kept her from dwelling on it. Penny was still attracted. But now she was determined to know more.

"I asked you something earlier," she said, piercing him with a stare. "I'm asking again, and I want to know the truth."

He adjusted the burner on the stove, then turned to give her his full attention. She thought she heard a sigh, as if he'd resigned himself to something unpleasant. And for a second, she almost didn't want him to answer.

Instinct told her the truth might be harder to handle than the curiosity. But curiosity won out.

"Tell me, Mr. Wolf. Who are you?" She took one small step closer. "Who are you, *really?*"

He didn't move, never shifted his gaze. Instead, after the slightest hesitation, he baldly answered her question.

"My name *is* Lucas Wolf. I am a lawman from Elatyria, a place you've probably considered fictional all your life. I'm one-quarter Wolf. And I've been hired by a queen to find you and bring you back to Riverdale."

She didn't respond. Didn't gasp. Didn't laugh in his face.

To be honest, she didn't react at all for a second. She merely stared at him, noting the stone-cold seriousness of his expression, replaying his voice in her head, trying to decide if he was delusional or merely pulling her chain.

Finally, though, she had to admit he wasn't playing some crazy joke. He might be nuttier than a jar of Skippy, but he believed what he was saying.

"Okay," she muttered, putting an end to an internal debate over whether she should call 911 or run out into the night. Doing neither, she instead walked over to open a kitchen cabinet and said, "I think we're going to need some tequila to get through the rest of this conversation."

HE KNEW from experience that this tequila she craved was a weak brew. Yet it seemed to brace the princess. Before she even opened her mouth to discuss the matter, she tossed back two small shots of the stuff. She shivered once, then dove right in.

"You're an escaped mental patient, right? Damn, I knew it."

He merely smiled.

"Come on, you *can't* expect me to believe this."

"I don't expect you to, which is why I wanted to take you and show you the proof rather than trying to explain it."

"Take me where, to this imaginary place called Riverdale? Or is it Elatyria?"

"Riverdale is a territory, what you'd call a country. Like these United States. It exists in the world of Elatyria, which borders this one that you call Earth."

"Oh, right." Sarcasm saturated her words. She was humoring him. "You're from another planet?"

"Hardly. Just because you Earth dwellers have explored space doesn't mean you know all there is to know about this world."

She merely stared.

Trying to put it simply, in the terms he'd first heard a few years ago when his completely unknown half-brother, Hunter, had come looking for him, he explained. "Think of it like this. Two lands occupying the same space, only…"

She interrupted again with a snap of her fingers and a grin. "Wait. You're telling me you're a time traveler? From the past?"

His eyes narrowing, he held back an instinctive growl. The woman was a pain in the ass. But damn, how he liked her.

"Do you want to hear this or not?"

She waved an expansive hand. "Oh, by all means! I'm truly fascinated, hanging on every word."

She couldn't have sounded more disbelieving if he'd told her he needed her to help calm a raging dragon hungry for a virgin princess. Not that Lucas necessarily believed that legend. He had always suspected the whole thing had been made up by some horny guy trying to get a princess to give it up. And though Penny was indeed a princess, he doubted she satisfied the other requirement.

That didn't thrill him, since he considered her his. Yet not being her first didn't enrage him either. He certainly couldn't claim inexperience. Only a hypocrite would blame her for being what she was—a passionate young woman—up until now.

Only one thing truly mattered. That he would be the *last* man ever to possess her.

"Hello? Taking a break to think up the rest of your tall tale?"

He blew out a harsh, frustrated breath, wondering how this woman had already worked his brain into a knot of confusing thoughts. "What I'm trying to say is that your world and mine co-exist, that they're simply separated by a few degrees of reality."

She snorted. "Yeah, well, I think you're separated from reality by about a hundred and eighty degrees, my friend."

Turning away from her, he grabbed the tequila bottle from the counter. He lifted it to his mouth and drained half of its contents into the back of his throat.

Not much better than water. But it had given him a second to keep himself from throwing the woman over his shoulder and kidnapping her in order to prove that what he said was true.

Calmed, he turned to face her again. "Neither Elatyria or Riverdale exist on any map in your world. Those who move back and forth between the lands don't speak of their travels for fear of being thought mad."

She mumbled something under her breath. Seeing his clenching jaw, though, she didn't repeat herself.

"But they do exist. Your own father lived at least ten years of his life over there." Lucas had done research on the family before he'd come here to track her down.

For the first time, the disbelief was replaced—briefly—by a hint of wonder. "Ten years?" She glanced past him, mumbling something under her breath. "He was missing for ten years…."

Sensing an opening, he pressed on. "You don't remember, but you've been there, too."

"What?"

"Your father never told you a thing about your childhood? The two of you lived in Riverdale until you were almost three."

She plopped onto a chair. "*Lived* there? Me and my father?"

"And your mother, of course. Where do you think they met?"

She caught her bottom lip between her teeth, thinking about it. Finally, she admitted, "He always said they met at NYU."

He tilted his head in confusion.

"New York Univ— Look, it doesn't matter. I went there. It wasn't true. There was no record that either of my parents studied there."

"Not surprising. I don't imagine there are any official documents about your mother in this world at all."

Her mouth dropped open in confirmation, but she just as quickly jerked it closed. "That doesn't mean anything."

"It's one more piece to the puzzle you've always wondered about, though, isn't it?" he asked, his tone reasonable, unthreatening.

She wasn't in the mood to be reasoned with. She shook her head, as if shaking off a hint of doubt. "You do know I'm on the verge of calling someone to take you to one of those places with rubber-walled cells, right?"

For all her protestations, Princess Penelope's eyes could not lie. They betrayed her. Right now, they swam not with disdain and disbelief, but with wonder. She was considering his story. Opening her mind. Perhaps because she'd already had questions about her parents, her mother. From the sound of it, she had gone looking for her history and hadn't found it.

Because it wasn't there to be found. At least, not in this world.

"According to legend, your father stumbled into the outer territories, a desert which bordered Riverdale. He was brought before your mother, half-dead, accused of being a spy. They say it was love at first sight."

Penny swallowed visibly. Then the hint of wonder left her. Correction: she forced it away, he saw it in the deliberate tightening of her lips. "This is such a load of crap."

"I know how it sounds," he insisted. "That is why you must come with me and allow me to prove it."

"Prove some other dimension exists? Yeah, right." He'd already noticed the way she immediately relied on sarcastic humor when she began to doubt. Now was no exception. "Are we going to run into the Jolly Green Giant there?"

"Giants aren't green. Nor are they *ever* jolly."

She leapt from her chair. "Oh, give me a freaking break."

He thrust a frustrated hand through his hair. It was like trying to tame a unicorn, leading her one step forward only to have her pull two steps away. "Princess…"

"What's with the princess stuff?"

"Your mother was Queen of Riverdale. You are her only surviving child. Her only heir. You *are* a princess."

Her lips twitched. Relieved laughter spilled out. "Oh, God, this is a joke! Who set this up, that witch Angie?"

He tensed. "You keep company with a witch?"

"Jeez, you don't give up, do you?"

"Witches are not to be trusted."

"I was kidding. I call her a witch instead of the word with a *b* because we're old friends."

"Don't joke about witches," he snapped, trying to slow his pulse and hide the fact that the hairs on his body were standing on end. Instant defense mechanism.

Gaping, Penny threw herself down into her chair again. "Gorgeous but insane. So sad," she mumbled. Scooping up a fork, she began shoveling greens from the salad he'd made her into her mouth, ignoring him.

He wished he could say he found his late-night repast as appetizing. A hot veggie burger was bad enough. A cold one was more than he could stomach.

Finally, after she'd devoured half her salad, she muttered, "So who's this queen who *supposedly* sent you?"

"Queen Verona," he replied, taking a seat opposite her. She was pretending she was only casually interested, as a way to kill time while she ate. He knew better. She was curious. Whether she wanted to be or not. "She and her family have been ruling Riverdale in your absence."

She must have heard his dislike for the queen. "Let me guess. This queen is a real witch, with the *b* though, right?"

He couldn't contain a faint smile.

"And she sent you, why?"

"I'm a lawman. I track people for a living."

She finally sighed. "You know, you are the sexiest guy I've ever met, and you saved my butt tonight. But I just can't believe anything you say."

"I know you don't want to."

"My father loved me." Her voice grew soft, as if she didn't mean to speak aloud. "He *would* have told me."

He heard the emphasis. "Yes. I'm sure he would have. Maybe he just didn't get the chance."

Penny's cheeks flushed. "It's crazy…"

"But not impossible." Lucas thought of her still-wrapped present. "You said he died before you turned twenty-one. What if that gift was something he intended to give you to help explain the truth? Maybe that's when he was planning to reveal all."

She snagged her bottom lip between her teeth, indecision stamped on her face.

"It might be time for you to open your present, Princess."

Penny didn't reply, a number of emotions undoubtedly surging through her. More of that wonder. Confusion. Doubt. Finally, though, it came down to one. The one he least wanted to see.

Stubbornness.

"You can't come in here and start ordering me around."

He sighed. *One step forward, two steps back.* "I wasn't trying to. It was a suggestion."

She mumbled something, sounding more annoyed than confused, then dug back into her salad. After a few more bites, she spoke again.

"Tell me about this one-quarter Wolf thing."

He had wondered when she would get to that.

"Is being in the Wolf family some big deal? Since you're

only one-quarter related to them, did you get disinherited or something?"

"You know that's not what I'm saying."

She froze.

"You *know*."

Penny lowered her fork to her plate, eyeing him closely. His long hair hanging over his shoulders, his face, his eyes, his beard. She dropped her attention to his arms, straining against the jacket that seemed to have shrunk since sunset. To the dark hair on the backs of his hands.

Then she looked at his face again. He intentionally smiled, baring his teeth. His white, gleaming teeth, always a little bit sharper by full moonlight.

She looked. She gulped. And she muttered, "Oh, fuck."

"The queen won't like such language."

She scooted her chair back at least a foot. "You're trying to tell me you're a...a werewolf?"

"There's no such thing."

Nodding quickly, she sighed in relief. "Right."

Poor girl, he almost hated to explain. "You humans over here call us werewolves. In truth, we're just part wolf. No *were* about it. We don't turn into murderous animals when the moon grows full." He glanced out the window at the night sky. "Though I can't deny we do enjoy the moonlight, and some of our genetic qualities become more prominent beneath its glow."

"Your family must own stock in Gillette."

Not knowing what she meant, he ignored her.

She licked her lips, those pretty, tempting lips. "So you're saying you're part wolf?"

He nodded. "My father, as well as the others in my clan, are descendants of a race of half-humans, half-wolves, and they almost always intermarry. Keeping the line pure."

"Pure wolf-man. Gotcha."

He ignored her sarcasm, knowing it was generated by shock. "My father fell for someone outside the clan."

"Uh-huh. Where was she from, the Land of Oz?"

Remaining patient, he answered, "No. But since my mother was fully human, I only have a quarter of that wolf ancestry."

She hesitated, then finally snapped her fingers and grinned. "Wait! I'm unconscious. That pig knocked me out when he slammed me into the ground, and this is a coma-induced hallucination."

He simply stared at her. She stared back, her smile slowly fading. Penny was grasping at straws, trying to find a rational explanation for something that didn't have one. At least, not according to her view of the world.

A view of the world she wasn't going to part with easily.

"No. No, no, no!" She thrust each word out harshly. Penny pushed back her chair, rising from it. "You need to leave now.

He stood as well. "To use your favorite word, no."

She backed up until she reached the counter and could go no further. "I mean it. Get out of here."

"Not until I make one thing clear," he muttered, following her across the kitchen, step by step.

Fear flitted across her face, but he couldn't make himself do as she asked. He couldn't leave her, giving her time to adjust. They didn't have time. Besides, tonight wasn't the kind of night when he could even *pretend* to be patient.

When he reached her, he inhaled deeply, smelling not just that hint of fear but more of that excitement. It made her body quiver and her lips tremble. Her hands were behind her, clenching the edges of the countertop.

"What do you need to make clear?" she whispered.

Her heart started pounding as he stalked her. He felt it— almost heard it—in the silent air, thick with so many layers of tension he'd have trouble counting them all. But she didn't try to run.

Because she wanted him still. That was causing the most tension of all. She desired him, as she had in her bedroom when he could have taken her, ridding them both of this insane need they'd aroused in one another at first sight. At least temporarily…until it swelled out of control again.

That would probably have taken less than an hour.

He couldn't do it then, because he hadn't told her the truth about himself. Now he had. Now, as they said over here, all bets were off. "I've told you who I am. What I am. Why I came here."

She opened her mouth as if to scoff, but no words emerged.

"What I *didn't* tell you is that from the moment I saw you at the diner, I knew."

"Knew what?"

He leaned in, filling his every breath with her, studying the curls drying softly around her face, the full, pouty lips, the dark-purple eyes.

She licked those perfect lips. "Knew *what*, Lucas?"

He put both hands on the counter behind her, trapping her in place. Leaning down, he brushed his cheek against her hair, then nibbled his way down the pierced curve of her ear, feeling a helpless shudder roll through her. With his lips against her earlobe, he finally answered her question in a low whisper.

"I knew I had to have you."

# 6

PENNY had to wonder: was it legal to have wild, crazy, up-against-the-refrigerator sex with an insane person?

Probably not. Or at least it wasn't appropriate.

*Screw appropriate.* She desired this man so much she would do violence on anyone who told her she couldn't have him.

"You're certifiable." She tilted her head, inviting him to move that warm mouth down her neck. "But I still want you."

More than wanted, she was *dying* for him. She was on fire, from her head to her toes. As he tugged the small earring on her lobe into his mouth and sucked lightly, she sighed, remembering how he'd pleasured her breasts.

"I know you do," he replied, doing what she'd hoped for, pressing those lips to her pulse point. "And I am still a wolf."

"Yeah, yeah, whatever," she muttered. "I guess that's a good thing. If you were a vampire I'd be in real trouble right now."

He lifted his head, looking down at her, passion blazing in his dark eyes. "Maybe you *are* in real trouble right now."

Penny sucked in a deep, excited breath as wanton heat roared through her. "I'm good at being in trouble."

He didn't hesitate, obviously hearing in her voice both an acceptance and a plea. Without warning, he picked her up by the waist, covering her lips in a deep, hungry kiss.

Penny groaned with pleasure, meeting his tongue, sucking it into her mouth. Wrapping her legs around his hips and her arms around his shoulders, she let everything go except this. This need, this wild hunger. Arousal tripped through her, setting each nerve ending afire until every inch of her burned and sparked.

Their kisses were consuming, devouring, and Penny felt lightheaded as he carried her to her bedroom. He didn't drop her onto the bed, but fell onto it with her. Their tongues dueled, wet and rough. She tasted every corner of his mouth, reveling in the flavors of him.

When his powerful hands moved to the hem of her T-shirt, Penny lifted up to help. Loving the way he had consumed her with his eyes before, she pulled her mouth from his, wanting to see every moment. They shared a deep, panting breath, and she watched him shift his gaze to her body, saw the way his eyes flared and his mouth fell open on a low groan as he tossed the shirt away.

"I like these," he admitted hoarsely, reaching to play with the rings on her nipples even as he lowered his mouth to one.

Penny hissed, stunned at how good it felt. Her breasts had always been sensitive, but this was beyond anything she'd ever experienced. She'd had the piercings done months ago after a breakup. It had been a crazy spur-of-the-moment impulse. Lucas was the first lover she'd had since. The overwhelming pleasure, with the tiniest hint of pain, as he suckled, tweaked and plucked had her digging her heels into the bed, arching toward his mouth.

It was exquisite, intense, and waves of delight began swirling to the core of her. The hard ridge of his erection pressed against her groin, and she bucked toward him. Each flick of his tongue took her higher, and she twined her hands in his thick hair, long and lustrous, soft against her bare skin.

But she couldn't hold him in place once he decided to move.

That was okay. Because he moved *down*.

"Oh, yes!"

Lucas was pulling her skirt off her before his mouth ever reached her waist. He dipped his tongue lower, into the hollow above her pelvic bone. Pulling back, he studied the tattoo on her hip. "A serpent?"

"Dragon," she admitted.

He shook his head. "That's a poor excuse for a dragon. You've obviously never seen one."

She let out a half laugh, half groan. "Would you shut up? I'm trying to forget that you're insane."

"I'm not insane." He licked the dragon's tail.

"I'm reserving judgment." She whimpered with pleasure. "Maybe you'll like one of my other tattoos better." She could think of one or two she'd like him to taste.

He scraped his tongue lower, against the elastic waistband of her panties. "Where are they?"

"You'll have to find out for yourself."

"I can hardly wait."

Holding her breath, she quivered as he ran his fingertips from her belly to her hip. He took her silky underwear along, too, exploring her with his mouth as he uncovered her.

When he noticed the miniscule thatch of curls, he paused. She *felt* him laughing against her skin even before she heard the low, wicked chuckle. "You lied."

"I don't use a razor," she insisted.

"My eyes, my mouth, my tongue, they all know better."

"It's called a Brazilian…." The explanation died in her throat. He wasn't listening, obviously didn't need to hear about her latest visit to a waxing salon. His satisfied expression and slow, reverent kiss on the bare lips of her sex told her everything she needed to know about how much he liked it.

"Oh, my," she whispered.

Slowly, with agonizing restraint, he began to explore her most intimate places. Lucas dipped his tongue deep to taste her body's essence. Her hips jerked, but he held her still.

"I like this," he mumbled.

"Ditto," she gasped. She wriggled toward him, craving more, needing that warm tongue to scrape across her most sensitive spot, knowing that as soon as it did, she would probably fly into a million pieces.

"I like it a lot."

She tried not to whimper. "Ditto a lot."

As he moved away and kissed the inside of her thighs, she heard another one of those evil, masculine chuckles and knew he was intentionally tormenting her.

"Do it, Wolf!"

He looked up at her with that white, gleaming smile. "Is that an order, Princess?"

She gulped, but not from fear. His hands holding her hips were strong, but not punishing. His mouth was teasing, not cruel. He was bringing her to amazing heights, and she knew, instinctively, that he would never let her fall. Never.

Her lips curling into a genuine grin, she whispered, "Let's call it a request."

"I can hardly refuse a royal request." His dark eyes gleamed, then he finally gave her what she needed.

Flicking his tongue over her clit, he teased and pleasured her until her body shook in a powerful climax. Penny had never been a screamer, but the absolute perfection of it brought a high-pitched cry to her throat and she had to release it.

He cut off the cry by covering her mouth with his, kissing her deeply, sharing the flavors of her own body. Penny wriggled beneath him, desperate to have him hot and naked against her. She didn't know whose hands pulled his T-shirt off. She only knew that within a second, a hard male chest was pressed against hers.

"Oh, Lucas," she mumbled, staring at him, the breadth of him. She also noted the ruggedness—a few scars that hinted at a rough past, the ridges of powerful muscle that no gym workout could ever provide. The dark, thick hair that proclaimed him all testosterone-laden male.

She gazed down, seeing the way it did, indeed, taper into a thin line. His jeans bulged where it disappeared, as if his erection was going to burst out the top. *God, he's huge.*

Reaching for him, greedy, needful, she whispered, "Please."

He didn't reply in words, just with a low, deep growl as he thrust into her hand. Penny reached for the zipper, not wanting denim fabric but the silky skin covering a rock-hard cock. In a moment, she had it, thick and immense. Every part of her that wasn't already wet melted into a puddle of pure sexual desire.

Lucas pulled away for a moment, long enough to kick off the rest of his clothes, then returned to settle between her thighs.

"Birth control?"

"Covered," she said, grabbing his hips and tugging him forward. "Please, Lucas, fill me up."

"With pleasure."

Despite his obvious hunger, he went slowly at first, as if worried he might hurt her. Even while almost cooing with pleasure at the feel of him sliding in, making a place for himself inside her body, Penny found herself amazed by his self-control. She could see the quiver of his every muscle as he strained to ease into her rather than thrusting hard, fast and deep.

But Penny wanted it hard, fast and deep.

"More!" she insisted, curving her hips up.

He groaned, and seemed to lose his ability to take it slow. As if the last tether had broken, Lucas drove into her, burying himself to the hilt. Penny threw her head back on the pillow, crying out as yet another orgasm washed over her.

Sex had never been like this. So intense. Earthy. *Delicious.*

"Perfect," he muttered against her hair, staying still.

*Perfect. Yes.*

He wasn't able to remain still for long. Murmuring heated whispers, he began to move, pulling away, emptying her, only to fill her, again and again, with long, devastating strokes. They found an immediate rhythm, totally in tune with each other, exchanging deep, ravenous kisses with every thrust.

Penny became lost to time, lost to place, lost to self. Nothing existed except the feel of him. His scent, his weight, his thickness, his groans of pleasure.

Finally, his climax. She felt it rise in him, felt the strain of his powerful muscles as he tried to fight it.

"Penny…."

"Yes," she cried, feeling, unbelievably, another climax

washing over her as well. And only when she was in the throes of it did he let himself go over, joining her in a soul-stirring moment of pure ecstasy that she sensed would be a turning point of her entire life.

THOUGH she had worked an eighteen-hour day, endured an assault, been told the mother of all bedtime stories, and had the most incredible sex of her life, Penny couldn't sleep.

Lucas didn't seem to have the same problem. He was lying beside her in the bed, naked, gorgeous, gleaming with sex-sweat. All hard, rugged male, still half-erect—*wow*—as if he were taking a break before starting all over again.

*Fine by me.*

But she didn't wake him up. She needed to catch her breath, not to mention get her thoughts in order. Her brain was going a mile a minute and she wanted to figure out what she'd done…and what she intended to do. About a number of things.

"Starting with you," she whispered, looking up at the shelf above her head. At the package. The last gift she would ever receive from the only parent she would ever know.

Since the day Callie had given it to her, she had never been tempted to untie the ribbon, or let her fingers tear through the paper. Any curiosity she'd felt had been overpowered by the need to hold on to her dad for a little while longer.

But you couldn't really hold onto things forever, could you? Not anything. Not jobs or homes or friends. Not loved ones.

Everything came to an end sooner or later. Journeys, relationships, lives. The echo of words left unsaid and the dreams of moments left unshared…all had to end eventually.

Knowing what she had to do, Penny sat up and grabbed the box. A kitchen light provided enough illumination, not that she needed it. She'd memorized the shape, the corners, each crease in the paper, each loop of the bow.

Her father had wrapped this final gift himself. She recognized the crooked seam, the overuse of tape. He'd written her name on the envelope and sealed it with love.

She couldn't open the card yet. Couldn't read his final words to her. That was one step beyond her capabilities.

Instead, she reached for the ribbon. Her hand seemed distant, far away, as if someone else was untying the bow. A drop of moisture appeared on the paper. Penny saw it, knowing, of course, that hers was the hand doing this heart-breaking thing she had tried to avoid. Hers were the tears marking the moment.

"I'm sorry, Dad," she whispered. "I miss you."

She pushed the paper off to reveal a plain cardboard box. Inside was a sea of tissue paper…and something that shimmered and gleamed. She immediately knew what it was. That gleam had been too bright to be anything but a precious stone, and the object too large to be a piece of jewelry. It was a crown. She didn't need to know anything about fairy tales to recognize that.

The thought that her father had been playing a practical joke occurred to her. But the crown was too heavy, and appeared too old. Ornate and intricate, it was made of some solid metal and decorated with dozens of jewels, including one enormous amethyst cut in the shape of a heart.

Tucked inside the box was a note. The handwriting was not her father's.

My Dear Penny—
Happy 21st birthday. I wish I could have been there to share this day with you, and so many before it. I love you so much. Please try on your gift and you'll see how much. It's belonged to the women of our family for hundreds of years.
With all my love—Mother

Even as sadness stabbed into her at seeing her mother's handwriting for the first time, she also felt a sudden, over-whelming sense of peace. Because, suddenly, she knew who she was. Where she came from, who her people were.

It was true. All true. Everything Lucas had said.

Although it was beyond belief, she could do nothing *except* believe. The proof was right here in her hands.

She glanced over at him, saw how still he was, how deep and even his breaths. How dark, dangerous-looking. Fierce. If the *rest* of the story was true….

*No. Don't even think about that. Not yet, anyway.*

It was one thing to have mentally acknowledged the almost animalistic strength of the man, the power, the sexual heat of him that was more potent than any human male she'd ever known. It was another to openly admit he was truly…what he clamed to be.

"Later," she mumbled. She'd think about it later.

There was something else she had to do first. Her mother had made a request of her. Grasping the crown, she lifted it toward her head. Emotions and fears, thoughts and wishes sped through her, and she already knew, somehow, that from this moment on, she was not going to be the same person, ever again.

She closed her eyes. And lowered the crown into place.

There was a charge of static, a jolt of energy. She almost yanked it back off, but before she could do it, a collage of images poured into her mind. "Oh, my God," she whispered, focusing on whatever magic was laying out these scenes.

First, a landscape, the grass so green it looked artificial. Here and there, spring flowers grew in scattered clumps— huge tulips and daffodils and some she couldn't name that were as big as dinner plates and as rich in color as the jewels on the crown.

Then someone came into focus. A small figure, dark-haired, running through the grass, carrying so many flowers she looked ready to fall over. When she did stumble over the hem of her long dress, a man swooped in to grab her and set her on his shoulders, both of them laughing as the blooms rained down on his head.

She knew him immediately, of course. "Dad," she whispered. He looked familiar, but not as she remembered him from his final years. Here he was vibrant, strong. Just a young man, untouched by the currents of life that would slowly drain his youth out from under him the way the tides took the sand.

He carried the child closer. Close enough for her to see the nearly black curls, the violet eyes, the slightly up-tilted nose.

She was seeing herself. But not as an impartial observer. It wasn't like looking at a photograph, or a home movie through the anonymous, impersonal perspective of a camera lens. Because as she looked at the father and child, she was suffused with such an overwhelming sense of love and gratitude, she *knew* she was seeing someone else's memories, feeling someone else's emotions.

Penny heard the echo of a woman's laughter. Then, in the movie of her mind, a slender hand reached out and touched the girl's soft cheek, smoothing the dark hair off the younger Penny's brow. A voice crooned something sweet. A lullaby that traveled through time, awakening the melody that had long been buried inside Penny's own mind.

Her mother's hand. Her mother's voice.

Her mother's gift.

"Penny?"

The images faded, as if the reel had come to its end.

"Penny, are you all right?"

She nodded, hearing Lucas's concern. Opening her eyes, she smiled at him. He sat beside her, watching her closely.

"I'm fine, Lucas," she admitted, meaning it. "And I'm ready to go with you as soon as you want to leave."

# 7

THEY GOT on the road by mid-afternoon.

After the long night of steamy sex and conversation, Lucas hadn't needed to press Penny to get an early start. The crossing to Elatyria was in a marsh between Baton Rouge and New Orleans. The journey on his bike took only a few hours.

They'd spent the morning getting ready for the trip, packing some clothes and Penny's crown in a small backpack. He didn't imagine she'd need the clothes for long...the crown was another story. While they packed, Penny asked a million questions about his world. He shared as much as he knew, including telling her about his family—his father and half-brothers. She'd been interested, but her questions hadn't delved too deeply into his gene pool. Not ready to go there yet, he supposed.

She had, however, wanted to hear more about his job. "So you hunt people, huh?"

"It's not so unusual. My human brother has a similar job over here. He calls himself a bounty hunter."

She eyed him thoughtfully. "Another brother?"

"Half-brother. We have the same mother. As I said, she was human, not a Wolf."

"What's *her* name, Helen of Troy?"

"You really don't know your stories, do you?" he asked with a grin. "The natural question would be to ask if her name was Snow White or Rapunzel."

"Sorry. Never had any use for fairy tales."

He didn't try to convince her that in his world, those fairy tales were called history. Once she got there, she'd see the proof. Like the statue honoring Queen Sin, a vicious bitch—with a definite *b*—with a glass-shoe fetish. Her story hadn't been as nice as the one the Grimms had told. There had been no pumpkin coach. And only one stepsister, who had lost her head sometime during Sin's reign.

The fairy godmother part, though, had been true. He'd often thought being a fairy godmother—granting the wishes of selfish, undeserving princesses and the like, without ever having one granted for yourself—had to be the worst job in *any* world.

"So your human half-brother lives over here all the time? How come?"

He quickly told her about Hunter and their mother. Including the fact that she had chosen to leave Lucas behind when she'd left Elatyria.

"How could she *do* that?" she asked, sounding stunned.

He shrugged, long since having gotten over any resentment. "She was miserably unhappy. But she knew my father and I would both be even more unhappy over here. I don't imagine it was easy for her."

Penny shook her head, sadness visible in her eyes. The princess would deny it but he knew she had a soft heart under that brazen shell.

Lucas quickly changed the subject, telling her more about Elatyria. Having had her mind opened to the existence of another world, she'd become voracious on the subject. He'd found himself dredging up old school lessons—things people over here had learned about in Disney movies. Except for Penny, who said she had never seen one.

There had only been one thing she'd asked about that he hadn't answered to the best of his ability.

"So what's the deal with this Queen Verona? If she's such a bitch and has control over some prime real estate that I might decide to claim, why'd she send you to find me?"

"Who knows why royalty does what they do?" he'd replied. "I'm just glad they occasionally *do* it."

Penny's wicked smile said she was distracted by the answer. As he'd intended.

He could have told her the truth. But admitting to a woman who'd slept in his arms last night that he was supposed to bring her home to marry another man didn't seem wise.

*It doesn't matter.*

There would be no marriage. Penny had given herself to him freely and Lucas wouldn't let her go. Not ever.

She was his now.

No, he hadn't had the chance to tell her that his kind usually mated once, for *life*. He'd intended to before taking her to bed, but the woman had so infuriated him, he hadn't gotten beyond his explanation of who he was and where he was from.

At least he'd told her that much.

They had time to get everything else in the open. After they made it through the border tonight, the last night of the full moon, they could slow down. Their journey to the castle could take as long as they damn well needed it to once they were across. He'd explain everything then.

And he'd make sure she never *wanted* to leave him.

"I feel so bad about leaving Callie in the lurch, though she was great about it," she said as she climbed up onto his Harley.

"She said last night she wanted you to go."

"You heard that? Our conversation?"

"Of course I did."

"You must have been close by."

He made sure she was firmly settled on the tiny back seat. "I was a block away."

Her eyes flared as she took that in, but she didn't respond. Penny seemed to have decided to deal with his wolfness by ignoring it for now.

That was all right. It was a lot to digest. She'd made it clear during the night that she wasn't bothered by his genetics. Because, even after she'd tried on her mother's crown and accepted everything he'd told her, she'd climbed on top of him and ridden him into near oblivion.

His mouth going dry at the memory of it, he ran a hand over his lips. His skin still carried her scent, as hers did his. They had marked each other, even if he was the only one who knew it.

"Ready?" he asked, knowing they had to leave before he did something stupid like drag her back inside for another game of let's-find-Penny's-tattoos. She had one on her hip, one on her ankle…and one left to find.

He hadn't done a thorough explanation of her back side. And he wanted to. Badly.

"*So* ready."

"Then let's go, Princess," he said as he climbed on.

She whacked him on the shoulder. "Don't call me Princess."

"Fine. But feel free to continue to issue royal requests. I like granting them."

Her shapely thighs, clad in black jeans that were more suited to the motorcycle than one of her skirts would have been, tightened around his hips and she slid closer. Her sex was pressed into his back and through their clothes, he felt an instant rush of heat.

She wouldn't object if they went back inside, either.

He ignored that thought. Smothering a groan, he kick-started the bike, suddenly wishing he had a car. Despite how much he hated being trapped inside one of the reeking machines, he had the feeling that flying down the highway with her sweet legs wrapped around him was going to be pure torture.

Over the next few hours, he was proven right. Penny curled herself around him, gripping him with her legs, her arms wrapped around his waist. Though the wind whipped across them wildly, he could still feel every inch of her and he *burned*.

"You probably shouldn't have told me how good your hearing is," she whispered against his neck as they neared the turnoff.

He didn't respond.

"Because I know you can hear me." Her warm lips pressed against the pulse below his ear. "I want you, Lucas."

He swallowed.

"I wish you had put me on your lap to straddle you. Mm, what I wouldn't give to feel your cock buried inside me as we ride and ride."

"Wench," he muttered.

"What?"

He didn't repeat it.

Her soft chuckle was decidedly evil. Her hand dropped to his lap and he quivered as she felt the way his body had responded to her words. He was rock-hard and ready.

"Or maybe I wouldn't have to straddle you," she added, stroking him lightly, maddeningly. "I could face away from you, lean forward over the handlebars, let you slide into me from behind."

He groaned. "God, woman, are you trying to kill us both?"

"I'm horny," she admitted with an impish chuckle.

"Hold that thought."

Taking the poorly marked exit almost without slowing, he skidded onto a back road that was rarely traveled. The bike didn't have much traction, spewing gravel in its wake, but he didn't slow down. Pure sexual energy drove him and the powerful engine between his legs only served to rev him up harder. As did the rising moon.

"Hurry." She sounded as desperate as he felt.

Night had fallen, the moon was full, the border open. But they had enough time. Just enough for what he wanted to do to her.

Spying the small, decrepit shack where he stored his bike and other belongings, he roared toward it. He had barely pulled up outside before Penny was shifting around, climbing onto his lap. She pressed her mouth to his, kissing him wildly, her small hands cool against his hot, windblown face. Writhing against him, she said, "Don't make me wait."

"I don't intend to."

Damn, of all times for her to give up her skirts. He hated wasting the precious seconds it took to tug her jeans open.

Kissing her again, he maneuvered the button and zipper until he could reach inside to touch her. Pushing her panties out of the way, he teased her hard little clit until she cried out. Penny was creamy with readiness, and she thrust against his hand, wanting more. He gave it to her, sliding his finger between her lips and into her tight channel.

"More, more," she mumbled, kissing his face, already pulling her shirt up and off.

He slid another finger into her, making love to her with deep, fast strokes, and she rocked back, taking every thrust.

Still not enough.

He wrapped an arm around her waist and stepped off the bike. Letting her go only long enough to shove his jeans down, he didn't waste time pulling them all the way off. Penny was faster, getting out of hers in an instant. Before he could even begin to ask her whether she really wanted *everything* she'd said she did, she turned around and bent over the seat of his bike, her gorgeous ass pale in the moonlight.

And he found her last tattoo.

She looked over her shoulder at him and licked her lips. "Please, Lucas."

He couldn't have said no if someone had set his legs on fire.

With the full moon raining down on him and every primal instinct screaming for release from their human constraints, he grabbed her hips and slid his erection between her curvy cheeks. She rubbed up and down in welcome, her body's juices flowing hot on his skin, sizzling in the cool nighttime air.

"This isn't going to last long," he growled through gritted teeth.

"I don't care. Give it to me!"

Rough, passionate, wild. Untamed.

He did as she asked, grabbing his thick cock in one hand, spreading her legs even wider for his penetration. Then he entered her, hard, deep. She cried out with pleasure, thrusting back, taking everything he had and obviously loving it. At the feel of her, silky smooth, steamy hot and so tight, Lucas could only throw his head back and let out a cry that would sound like a howl to anyone close enough to hear.

But there was no one. Just him and Penny, thrusting wildly under the stars, lost in lust and sensation and pleasure.

He didn't climax as fast as he'd feared, but it didn't take long. Feeling it build, he tried to slow, not wanting it to end, not wanting to leave her unfulfilled.

She, however, wouldn't let him change the pace. "Don't you dare." Her body pulled him deep inside, milking, squeezing, egging him on, until, helpless to do anything else, he came in a hot rush, flooding her with his seed.

He howled again, but even while lost in the throes of pleasure, he had no intention of leaving Penny hanging. Still inside her, he wrapped an arm around her waist, pulling her up to stand before him, his front pressed to her back. He kissed her neck, ran one hand up to cup a beautiful breast and tweak it. The other he dropped to her sex, stroking her clit until she exploded.

"Oh, Lucas!"

The strength seemed to leave her legs and she collapsed back against him, but he didn't let her fall. Holding her close, he continued to kiss her, caress her, feeling her heart begin to slow and her panting breaths begin to ease.

"Thank you," he whispered against her nape.

"For what?"

"For helping me find your last tattoo."

She laughed and wriggled against him. "Believe me, I didn't know it was called a tramp stamp when I had it done. I'm really not the type to go around advertising that I'm easy."

"You're not easy," he whispered.

*You're mine.*

LUCAS HAD CALLED it a border. So Penny had been picturing an invisible line, one that didn't really exist anywhere but on a map drawn by some surveyor. He *hadn't* said it was an actual physical barrier that would make her feel as though she was plunging through a thick layer of wet spiderwebs.

As Penny followed him through the cloying, reeking tangle

of Spanish moss that somehow wasn't *really* moss, she wrinkled her nose and tried not to breathe. His hand was wrapped tightly around hers, and she knew he wouldn't let her go. Which was good, because even after getting through the moss, the air itself seemed to push back against them.

Crossing this border wasn't about moving through some low-hanging tree branches. Though not visible, or what she'd call solid, the separation between his world and hers was tangible.

She gasped with relief when they finally pushed out into clear, fresh air. The *freshest* air she'd ever inhaled, sweet and flavored with some spice that seemed like it belonged in a bakery instead of out in the wide open spaces.

"Welcome home," Lucas said, reaching up to push a few stray twigs from her hair.

Home. Just like that?

She didn't reply at first, slowly shifting her gaze to study her surroundings. The differences between the world she knew and this one were not stark. Despite the smell—Cloves? Nutmeg?—this actually looked much like any small stand of woods. The thing was, a minute ago, she hadn't *been* in woods. She'd been standing in a swamp, hearing the croak of 'gators and the hum of mosquitoes.

"It's lovely," she admitted, wondering why she could so easily see the trees, the layer of pine needles on the ground. Then she realized it was because the sun was already rising. "Wait, how wide is that crossing? Is it morning?"

"Time is different over here. The days are shorter. You'll get used to…"

"Halt! Stop and pay the queen's toll!"

Shocked to hear another voice out here in the woods at the break of dawn, Penny could only stare as a figure emerged from between two trees. A diminutive man wearing rough-hewn clothes and a long cap sauntered closer. When he reached them, he hopped onto a stump and extended his hand, palm up, as if he expected it to be filled with money.

Lucas sneered. "What the hell do you think you're doing?"

"Collecting the queen's toll from every traveler," the frowning man replied. Rising on tiptoe, he glared directly into Lucas's face, which meant he had some major balls for one so small. "Now pay up or you won't be allowed to trespass across Riverdale."

Realizing they were indeed being asked to pay a toll by a grumpy dwarf, Penny could only stare, her mouth hanging open.

"Get out of my way. No Wolf pays a toll to a queen, especially one who isn't the rightful ruler of Riverdale."

"Wait! Are you the lawman?" The dwarf lifted a pair of thick spectacles to his eyes and peered through them owlishly. He studied Penny's face, focusing on her eyes, then stumbled, almost falling off his perch. He put his fingers in his mouth and let out a shrill whistle, then shrieked, "They're here!"

A sudden pounding echoed. Before Penny had time to process that she was hearing the sound of men running, she saw several of them in dark uniforms appear from the treeline.

Lucas instantly went on the defensive, grabbing her by the arm and shoving her behind him. "That double-crossing bitch," he snarled.

Penny realized they might be in real trouble. "The queen?"

"She might have decided it was easier to get rid of you! Damn, how could I have trusted her? I'm sorry, Princess."

She gulped, wondering if there was any chance the border was still crossable, despite the sun rising in the western sky…*western?* But before she could make a dash for it, dragging Lucas with her, the dwarf hopped off the stump and dropped to one knee before her.

"May I be the first to welcome your highness to Elatyria?"

Lucas hesitated, though she still felt the tension in his rock-hard form. "What?" he asked.

The dwarf ignored him, staring only at Penny. "We've been expecting you. Welcome."

"Uh, thanks," Penny said, looking to Lucas for guidance.

He visibly relaxed. "Sorry," he muttered. "I overreacted. It appears Queen Verona is welcoming you with open arms."

Rather than swords and executioners. Check.

Before she could reply, the guards converged on them. Surrounding her, they pushed between her and her escort.

"Your majesty!" the one in front said, bowing deeply. "Queen Verona sends her fondest welcome and is greatly looking forward to meeting you."

"Yeah, well, we'll get there," Lucas said.

"Please come with me, your majesty," the lead guard said, taking Penny by the arm. "We have a carriage ready for you and have been instructed to bring you to the palace immediately."

"Damn it," Lucas muttered.

Penny blinked, shaking her head, still a little dazed from the rough border crossing. And from the unexpected welcoming party.

From the way Lucas had talked, she'd expected to have another day or two alone with him: Taking their time making their way to the palace. Stopping to explore, touch, have wild, lovely, delicious sex. Even time to deal with the feelings they seemed to be rousing in each other so suddenly, so unexpectedly.

She didn't believe in love at first sight, despite what Lucas had told her about her parents. But something was there, something solid, sure. And growing. She wanted time to deal with it, to nurture it, before confronting the rest of her new life.

Lucas had seemed to desire the same thing. He'd told her he wanted to explain everything in more detail, prepare her for what was to come. Discuss the future.

Now, though, as she was being firmly escorted toward a gleaming carriage standing behind six white horses, she saw that fantasy slip away. Lucas was disappearing behind her, surrounded by a trio of guards, all of them looking belligerent and ready to stop him if he came after her. Indeed, when he stepped forward, he was grabbed by each arm.

Hell, if she ever needed to play the princess card, it was now. "Halt! Unhand my escort," she shouted, wondering how she'd found the words when what she'd really wanted to say was, "Dudes, hands off the merchandise."

The guards immediately dropped their arms, but didn't move out of Lucas's way so he could join her at the steps of the carriage. He stared at her from yards away, his brown eyes glowing with anger, frustration. Emotion.

"Your majesty," said the head guard, his voice low and urgent, "I know you felt secure in the company of the…Wolf. However, you are now in our custody. You're safe, I assure you."

She gritted her teeth, furious on Lucas's behalf about the inherent racism. "He's with me."

"He will be well-paid for his service. But, majesty, you must see that he cannot accompany you to the palace."

"Why the hell not?"

The guard seemed startled by her language. "Well, uh…because word that you've been traveling alone with a…man…would not make the best impression on the people, majesty. And it will almost certainly displease your future mother-in-law, the queen."

Penny froze, staring at him, trying to figure out if he'd really said what it had sounded like he'd said.

"Penny!" Lucas called.

He was still blocked by the guards, one of whom snapped, "She's your majesty to *you*, Wolf!"

"Now we must hurry," said the guard. "Your fiancé, Prince Ruprecht, has been so anxious to meet you."

Okay. He *had* said what it had sounded like he'd said.

"Wait," she whispered. "Just wait one damn minute."

She stayed still, her hand on the side of the beautiful gold-trimmed carriage, a few feet from the white horses who pawed the ground in anticipation.

She was a world apart from everything she'd ever known. Separated from everyone she'd ever held dear. Except one person. The person she had entrusted to bring her here.

He stood across the clearing, watching her, saying nothing. Penny stared at him, silently demanding the truth.

His jaw clenched and his eyes closed briefly. That was all the truth she needed.

The son of a bitch really had brought her here to marry another man.

# 8

NOT HAVING the luxury of a horse-drawn carriage, Lucas arrived at the castle one day after Penny did. In that time she had already started the entire court talking. The whispers were thick, every person having something to say about the long-lost princess.

*That hair! The clothes! Those rings on her ears! But the prince—he's enamored, can you believe it? He can't take his eyes off her.*

*Those* rumors he could have done without.

If he'd had any idea he and Penny would be separated as soon as they reached Elatyria, Lucas would have told her everything she needed to know before they'd crossed over. He'd never dreamed Queen Verona would recognize Penny as the princess without even meeting her. Was she so desperate to marry Ruprecht off that she'd accept Penelope Mayfair sight unseen?

*Of course she is.*

He'd been stupid, careless. And now, he might pay the ultimate price for that stupidity. Because the look of betrayal on Penny's face before the guards had tucked her into the carriage and driven her away had stabbed him right through the heart.

She might never forgive him. God, she might actually marry Ruprecht.

"No," he mumbled as he made his way through the throne room, thick with sycophants who wanted to get in the good graces of the princess they were so gleefully gossiping about.

He spotted her immediately. Penny had been changed out of her regular clothes and put into a formal gown that looked stiff and uncomfortable. It covered her up from neck to toe, revealing not a hint of ink on her skin, much less the bump of two silver hoops on her perfect nipples.

Beside her, sitting stoic and rigid on her throne, was Queen Verona. The queen's famed ivory skin now verged on puce and she looked ready to choke on her own tongue.

And the reason was obvious; Prince Ruprecht looked utterly besotted. He sat beside Penny, their hands entwined, their heads together as they whispered and laughed.

Lucas's heart pounded in his chest and his fingers curled into fists. He had never considered the prince any kind of competition, but now, Ruprecht and Penny looked like a happy, engaged couple.

*How could she?*

The thought quickly shifted. *How could* you, *fool?* Because the whole thing was entirely his fault for not telling her everything from the start.

"Lucas Wolf! The Huntsman!" a courtier announced.

Penny stiffened; he saw the way her spine went straight and her hand stilled. But she didn't acknowledge him at all.

Queen Verona, however, did. She jerked up from her throne, breaking all protocol by marching toward him. Ignoring everyone around them, she snapped, "You're sure *that* is the girl?"

"Quite sure, majesty," he said, knowing Queen Verona hated Penny already.

The queen closed her eyes and groaned softly. "My God, what have you led me to, Wolf?"

"Nothing but what you asked for," he replied evenly. "And I expect to be paid the agreed-upon price for doing my job."

Not that he really wanted the money or the land...not for himself at least. But if this whole situation was going to leave him alone for the rest of his life, having lost the woman he should have spent it with, the very least he could do was fulfill his promise to his father.

"My son can't marry *her.*"

Lucas frowned as Penny and Ruprecht laughed together over some shared joke. "I think he might argue that."

The queen's lip trembled. "She *can't* be the princess."

"She is, any test would prove it, I'm sure. Now, my purse?"

The queen froze, staring at him searchingly. "A test…"

Hell. "Majesty, there is no doubt. One need only look at her eyes…"

The woman waved a heavily ringed hand. "Coincidence." Then a crafty smile widened her lips and she turned in a broad circle to look at her son and his chosen princess. "My dear," she said, her voice ringing across the court, "there is one *minor* formality we must complete before we can proceed."

Penny finally looked up and Lucas would swear she intentionally avoided meeting his stare. But her smile was tight, her slim shoulders stiff as she raised an inquiring brow. "Yes?"

Queen Verona cast a knowing, conspiratorial smile at her courtiers. "We, of course, have to satisfy all the traditional requirements. Which means, my dear, that we must put you to the test."

A FRIGGING PRINCESS test? Who ever heard of *that?* For the first time ever, Penny found herself wishing she'd actually read a fairy tale once in her life. Not because she wanted to pass the test. Hell, no. Because she wanted to make sure she *didn't.*

She could fool a lot of people…but she could never fool herself. From the minute the carriage had pulled away from Lucas the previous morning, all she had been able to think about was getting back to him. First, to kick his butt for being so sneaky about his real motivation for coming to find her. Second, to find out how he really felt about her.

And third, to make sure he didn't get away.

She wanted him. More, she didn't want to ever be *without* him. If that equaled love at first sight, or love within twenty-four hours, then so be it. She'd call it love. She didn't need to put a name on it, she just knew she had to have the man in her life.

He felt the same way. No, he'd made no effort to approach

her this afternoon, but he'd burned her with a succession of
fierce, possessive glances. *Claiming* her.

He might have been sent to bring her back for Ruprecht.
But there was no doubt in her mind that Lucas Wolf wanted
her for himself.

"You're looking pale, my dear Penelope. Are you sure you
can go through with this?"

She looked at Prince Ruprecht, who was charming, if a bit
dim. He was leading her to the royal ballroom, where the big
princess test was to be conducted. Wondering how on earth
the dude hadn't yet figured out what he *really* wanted, she
replied, "Yeah, I'm sure. It'll be fine, don't worry."

"I *am* worried," he insisted. "What if you pass the test?"

Prince Ruprecht was on board with Penny's plan to throw the
contest. He didn't want to marry her any more than she wanted
to marry him, even though they had immediately hit it off. He
was funny, had a cutting sense of humor, and did a great impression of his bitchy mother. The perfect guy friend, actually.

As so many gay men were.

Not that he actually *knew* that about himself yet.

"Well, you still don't *have* to marry me. You can refuse me."

"But she'll only complain I'm too picky," he said with a
sigh. "I don't understand why I simply can't fall in love. But
I *like* you better than anyone I've ever met. So maybe we
should get married."

"I don't think so, Princey." Patting him on his arm, she said,
"Don't let her bully you. You should go live your life for
yourself rather than doing what your mother wants you to do."

His eyes widened and he stopped short of the closed
ballroom doors. "What else is there for me to do?"

"Oh, you might be surprised. I know of a place where you
could find everything your heart desires. It's a beautiful city
on a glimmering sea, with a golden bridge."

He looked fascinated. "A bridge of gold?"

"Well, no, it's not *really* gold, it's red. But they call it the
Golden Gate." She waved her hand in the air, drawing a word

picture for him. "And in this city, there is a great love of rainbows. They have a whole parade to celebrate their rainbow pride, and I guaran-damn-tee you, Ruprecht, if you go to it, you will absolutely find your heart's true desire."

He nodded, appearing fascinated. "I wish to hear more about this city on the morrow."

"It's a deal," she said.

Though, if she had her way, she wouldn't be here "on the morrow." Once she got this test business over with, and gained her freedom from any engagement, she intended to go after that stubborn Wolf. Once she'd straightened his butt out and got him to admit he couldn't live without her, they could figure out what she wanted to do about her kingdom.

Test or no test, if she decided she wanted to claim Riverdale, Queen Verona was in for one knock-down, drag-out bitch-slapping fight.

Penny had proof of her claim—her father's letter, which she had finally opened the previous night in the quiet of her castle chambers. She'd cried for hours after reading his words, which confirmed everything she'd learned about her past, her life, her history. She didn't want to share the note with anyone, least of all Queen Verona, but if it came down to a battle, she knew her father would want her to do whatever she had to. And he'd be cheering her on as she did it.

Penny was smiling at the thought as they neared the closed doors to the ballroom. Verona's castle was old and drafty, with thick stone walls and damp floors. If the concept of electricity had made it over here, it hadn't hit the royal digs yet.

From what Ruprecht had told her, the smaller palace at Riverdale was much better. Newer, more modern. Probably her father's doing, she thought, smiling.

She almost felt him here with her, and her mother, too.

"Here we go," the prince said as they reached the entrance and waited for the immense doors to be opened. Announced as a couple, they took a few steps inside, but then halted, both spying the monstrosity in the middle of the ballroom floor.

Mattresses. A veritable mountain of them.

"Oooh, I know this one!" Ruprecht hissed, clutching her arm.

But before he could fill her in, Penny was grabbed by Queen Verona, who dragged her forward and waved for silence. "Here is our precious Penelope, ready to begin her test." She gestured toward a tall ladder, which stood against the cloud-high bed. "Up you go, my dear!"

That was when Penny realized she was supposed to *sleep* on the damn thing. "You want me to climb up there?"

"Yes, indeed," the queen said, pushing her forcibly toward the ladder.

Okay, what was she supposed to do...prove she could float down as light as a feather or something princessy? Be able to dress in a ball gown while her head touched the ceiling? Be all gracious and royal about getting the shittiest guest bed in the castle? What the heck were princesses good for, anyway?

She didn't know, and there was nobody she could ask.

Absolutely nobody on her side. A quick look around the room confirmed it. Lucas wasn't here.

He wouldn't want to watch this. She knew him well enough to know that. But had he left for good? Gone back to his homeland, to his people?

Drat the man for making this difficult. She was the wronged party—he should be here all prostrate with grief. Or at least glaring at her and ordering her to forgive him or something.

*Maybe he doesn't want your forgiveness.*

*Maybe he doesn't want you.*

"Not worrying about that now," she mumbled. She had enough to think about, figuring out this test.

The entire court watched in titillated silence as the queen nudged Penny up the ladder. The only one who looked the least bit sympathetic was Ruprecht, who was mouthing something. He appeared to be asking her if she needed to go for a pee-break before bed.

Oh, yeah, that'd be real classy.

Finally, Penny reached the very top of the ladder, and

clambered onto the top mattress. It swayed only a little. And she had to admit, it was about the most comfortable surface she'd ever been on. If she actually intended to get some sleep tonight, she could think of worse places to do it.

"All right up there?" the queen shouted from below.

Penny peered over the side, gave the woman a thumbs-up, winked at Ruprecht and called, "Goodnight!"

*Now get outta here so I can figure this thing out.*

Fortunately, this test didn't involve an audience. Because Penny got her wish. The ballroom began to empty. Everyone drifted out, heads together in whispers, giddy laughter floating up to the ceiling.

The queen had Ruprecht by the arm and was tugging him with her, not about to let him stay and influence the competition. What, did Verona think he wanted Penny to *pass?* Because she had no doubt the queen wanted her to fail. If that hadn't been loathing in her eyes when she'd first set eyes on Penny's spiked hair and tattoos, it had come pretty close.

Just before sweeping out with a swish of her obnoxiously fussy gown, the queen paused to speak to a couple of those rough-looking guards. Two of them were stationed outside the doors, keeping everybody else out. And her in.

Then those doors slammed shut. She was alone.

She waited in silence, counting to a hundred. There was no rush—she had all night to go on the prowl for an answer to the test. Finally, when a few minutes had passed and she felt confident she wouldn't be interrupted, Penny sat up and pushed back the covers to climb down.

Then she suddenly realized she couldn't. Because a quick glance confirmed something she hadn't even considered.

The ladder was gone. The sneaky bastards had whisked it away while she'd been waving goodnight.

"Oh, great, now what am I gonna do?"

The question had been a rhetorical one. And yet, someone answered.

"Well, Princess, I'd say you should make very good use of this comfortable pile of mattresses."

Penny's heart raced as it flooded with excitement. Her body reacted to his voice, his scent, his aura, even before she saw him end his climb up the mattress mountain and emerge on the side of the bed.

"Lucas," she whispered.

Want and hunger and sweet emotion washed over her and she acknowledged that everything was going to be all right. Because he hadn't left. He was here. Ready to fight for her.

To claim her.

But she didn't intend to make it easy. The moment he clambered up onto the top mattress and knelt beside her, she fisted her hand and punched him in the shoulder. "You jerk!"

He grabbed her by the arms and hauled her against his chest, burying his face in her hair. His voice thick with emotion, he muttered, "I'm sorry, Princess. I was going to tell you, long before I brought you here."

"Yeah, yeah, I figured that much out already." She cooed a little as he ran his big, strong hands down her body, touching her all over as if he wanted to make sure she hadn't been hurt since they'd last been together.

She hadn't been. Not physically. Her heart? That *had* hurt for a little while, until she'd put it all in perspective. Still, she wasn't about to let him off the hook that easily.

"Tell me how you feel about me," she ordered.

He pulled back to stare down at her, the handsome, rugged face looking haggard, as if he hadn't slept or eaten. "What?"

She lifted a hand to his cheek, scraping her fingertips across the rough stubble. "How do you feel about me, Lucas?"

He shrugged and answered as if it were the most simple question in the world. "I want you for my own, for the rest of my life, Penny. I don't know what to call these feelings you bring forth in me, other than a certainty in my soul that we are meant to be together. And that if I were to lose you, I would never feel whole or happy again."

A smile tugged at the corners of her mouth. Because some words were just better than *I love you*. Some vows more binding, some emotions more deep.

"All right then," she murmured, smiling at him, happier than she'd ever felt in her life. "You'd better help me get down from here so we can make our getaway before morning!"

He shook his head and pushed her back down into the pillows, nuzzling at her neck. "I don't think so."

"Lucas," she groaned, "we don't have time."

He ran his tongue along the lobe of her ear, nibbling, blowing at the sensitive skin. "There's always time for this."

She sighed, pressing up and parting her arms and legs in welcome. "Maybe a quickie…"

"Huh-uh. You draping yourself over my Harley was as much of a quickie as my heart can take this week. We're going slow."

His words were both a threat and a promise. And he proceeded to make good on them, kissing and caressing her until she could think of nothing but him. His warmth, his touch.

When she urged him on, he forced her to wait, each stroke deeper than the last, each touch more erotic, yet infinitely tender.

He worshipped her body, showed the kind of restraint she didn't think any man could ever have. He also showed her that even though she loved him driving into her in a frenzy, a slow, gentle penetration was pretty damn fantastic, too.

With arms and legs entwined, mouths exchanging kiss after kiss, they rocked together on the top of the crazy bed, swaying and loving until she started to cry at how *lovely* it was. How beautiful and perfect.

"I'm going to love you all the days of my life," she whispered against his neck, knowing the confession ran counter to every rational thought she'd ever had.

She also knew it was true.

Finally, after he'd taken her flying far beyond the confines of this one room again and again, Penny felt him give himself over to his own climax. He shuddered as he came inside her, and she held him tight, feeling their hearts pound as one for several long moments. Then he rolled to his side, taking her with him, holding her as if he would never let her go.

Penny burrowed her face in his neck. "That was wonderful."

"I know."

*Arrogant man.*

"But we don't have much time to figure out this test."

"What?"

"I mean, I need to know what, exactly, I'm being tested on."

He let out a bark of laughter. "Good grief, woman, you really don't know your fairy tales, do you? This one is a classic. Everybody knows it."

"Okay, so explain, Mr. H. C. Andersen."

He did, telling her exactly what was going on in a few words, which left her gaping in shock.

"You're telling me there's a *pea,* one single *pea,* way down at the bottom of this bed, and I'm supposed to be so tender-skinned and delicate, it's gonna keep me up all night?"

He nodded once, his chest rumbling with laughter.

"I think I'm gonna barf. I *hate* princesses."

"I don't," he admitted, tugging her tighter against him. "At least, not all of them."

She kissed his lips quickly, then said, "Okay, babe, time to hit it. We have to get out of here. Otherwise, I'm going to be stuck trying to pretend I had a blissful night's sleep when really I was up all night being thoroughly done by the big bad wolf."

He swept a possessive, proud hand down her body. Then as if realizing what she'd said, he drew back to look at her closely. "Why would you need to do that?"

"So I can fail, of course." At his confused expression, she added, "I'm not going to marry Prince Ruprecht!"

"Of course you're not. You're going to marry me."

Not exactly a standard proposal. But she'd take it. She'd definitely take it. "Right, but I have to get out from under Queen Witchy Poo first."

"Ahh." He drew away from her a little to sit up. "I have to

tell you something. I've been doing some research. Asking a lot of questions. I even went to an ancient monastery to get some answers from the wise men this afternoon."

She tilted her head, waiting.

"Penny, do you know what a matriline is?"

"No."

"It's a monarchy in which the title and power passes *only* through the female line of descendants."

"Like in ancient Egypt?"

"Yes." He took her hand. "And in Riverdale."

She began to see where he was going.

"There is always a Queen of Riverdale, but never a King. Only a consort, like your father."

"Meaning Prince Ruprecht…"

"Can never be King of Riverdale. The power is *entirely* yours."

"I'm liking this concept," she admitted. Nibbling her bottom lip, she asked, "But are you okay with it? I mean, can you stand me being your boss?"

He laughed deeply, throwing his head back. "Sweetheart, you can boss around the entire world, but behind our closed bedroom door, we'll both know *exactly* how things stand."

She shivered a little, seeing that sexy, predatory gleam in his eyes. She might claim a kingdom. But every night, her wicked wolf would claim the queen.

Suddenly growing serious, he added, "Are you certain you want to deal with the stigma of being with a Wolf?"

She rolled her eyes and grunted, tempted to punch him again. "I think prejudice is going to be one of the first things we tackle once we get things back on track." Grinning impishly, she added, "That and indoor plumbing."

"One of the best aspects of your world," he agreed, kissing her temple. "To make it clear, once you are acknowledged as the true Mayfair princess, nobody can force you to do anything, *ever* again."

Including Queen Verona.

"So all I have to do is get her to acknowledge me as a true princess in front of the court? Then I can tell her to kiss my…"

"Yes."

Penny smiled, seeing exactly how to proceed.

Leaning toward the foot of the bed, Lucas grabbed a small backpack he'd dropped there. She hadn't even noticed it. "I thought you might need this." He reached inside it and withdrew her mother's crown.

Penny took it from him but didn't put it on her head. Not yet. She'd have it on in the morning when she climbed down to claim her kingdom.

And from that moment on, she'd fill the crown with her *own* lovely thoughts, wishes and dreams. Images of her loving husband, her beautiful children. Her happy life.

All of which she would have with Lucas Wolf.

# *Epilogue*

THE COURT was agog.

Never had they seen such a pure, vulnerable, tender-skinned princess. For when Penelope Mayfair descended from her tower of mattresses the morning after her ordeal, she looked frail, pained and weak. Her brilliant purple eyes—so like all the Mayfair women's—were luminous and moist, the dark circles beneath them telling the tale of her long, miserable night.

While she had appeared foreign and different on her arrival, now *everyone* looked and saw only the true, rightful daughter of the late Queen Lenore. The long-lost, but well-remembered crown on her beautiful head underscored that point.

Those closest to the damsel felt their hearts twist as they noted the redness of her skin, the faint marks on her throat and her shoulders. She walked carefully, as if her poor limbs were weak.

All those who hailed from Riverdale felt a stirring of anger at the treatment of their princess.

"Poor little thing," they whispered, all wanting to wrap her in the softest silk and comfort her.

The girl slowly made her way across the ballroom, members of the court melting away to let her pass, offering bows and murmured blessings.

Finally, she drew within a few feet of the queen, who was unable to take her eyes off the famous Mayfair crown.

"Queen Verona," Penelope exclaimed in a loud voice, "what have I done to offend you? How could you treat me like this?"

The queen froze.

"I never imagined that I, the last remaining member of the

royal family of Riverdale, would be treated in such a way. Asked to sleep upon a bed stuffed with boulders? I don't know that I shall *ever* recover."

Every bit of color disappeared from the queen's face. The court held its breath, knowing what this meant.

The princess had passed the test.

The two women eyed one another, and those present that day later swore they could almost feel an imperceptible shift of power. An acknowledgement by the old queen that she had been bested. The gauntlet thrown by the young one, letting everyone know she was a new force to be reckoned with.

At last, Queen Verona bowed her head briefly and murmured, "My deepest apologies."

The dark-haired girl smiled beneficently. "Ahh, well, I'm sure with the friendship between our two countries, it was nothing but a misunderstanding. When you visit us at our castle at Riverdale, we will assuredly offer you the finest of beds."

Queen Verona hesitated, appearing confused. Finally, though, she could deny the girl's heritage no longer. She was caught in a princess-test trap of her own making.

"I look forward to many such visits between our realms…uh…*Princess* Penelope."

And it was done. The greatest queen in Elatyria had acknowledged Penelope Mayfair as the true Princess of Riverdale. Its future queen. None could ever naysay her again.

The older woman, still appearing shaken, beckoned forth her son, the frowning Prince Ruprecht.

Princess Penelope, however, held up a hand before either of them could speak. "I must tell you now. There will be no betrothal," she said. "Where I grew up, people decide who they *want* to marry and such affairs of the heart are best left to the two people involved."

"Hear, hear," mumbled the prince.

"Ruprecht, you have my hand in friendship for as long as you desire it," she said, before turning her attention back to the queen. "Now, I must depart. My kingdom has awaited my attention long enough, though, of course, I thank you for overseeing it during my absence."

A ripple of laughter slid through the crowd as Queen Verona's skin turned a mottled red. It grew when Prince Ruprecht chuckled, seeming well-pleased by the turn of events. Only those closest heard him lean over to Princess Penelope and prattle something about longing to set off to find a bridge of gold and a parade of rainbows.

And then, as legend tells, the graceful, gracious young princess turned and nodded to the court. Every person dropped in a bow or a curtsey, watching while she strode toward the exit, looking every inch the royal being she was.

She paused only once. There, with a whisper, she took the arm of a dark, handsome man whose eyes blazed with devotion. He was a stranger, recognized by only a few at court, but obviously very well known by their princess.

The unquestionably beautiful couple smiled at one another. Exchanged an intimate glance. A brief touch.

Then the two of them walked out of the castle into the bright sun dawning over another glorious Elatyria day.

\* \* \* \* \*

*Wait! There are more adventures to be had
in the mystical land of Elatyria!*

Prince Ruprecht has run off to chase golden bridges and
rainbows, leaving no one to run his kingdom. And when a
female warrior sets off after the prince, she finds him unwilling to return.

Fortunately, though, the prince has a lookalike in this strange
new world: a construction worker who's willing to go along
for a ride to a castle…if it gives him a shot with the sexy
Amazon woman who's desperate for his help.

*It's the Prince and the Pauper…Blaze style!
Coming from Leslie Kelly
in BLAZING BEDTIME STORIES, VOLUME 5
May 2010!*

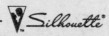

# Silhouette Desire

## FROM *NEW YORK TIMES* BESTSELLING AUTHOR

# DIANA PALMER

## THE MAVERICK

### A BRAND-NEW LONG, TALL TEXAN STORY

SD76982

# HARLEQUIN® HISTORICAL:
## Where love is timeless

**From chivalrous knights
to roguish rakes, look for the
variety Harlequin® Historical
has to offer every month.**

**www.eHarlequin.com**

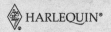

HARLEQUIN®

# INTRIGUE®

## FIRST NIGHT

BY

# DEBRA WEBB

To prove his innocence, talented artist
Brandon Thomas is in a race against time.
Caught up in a murder investigation,
he enlists Colby agent Merrilee Walters
to help catch the true killer. If they can survive
the first night, their growing attraction
may have a chance, as well.

*Available in December wherever books are sold.*

# REQUEST YOUR FREE BOOKS!

## 2 FREE NOVELS
## PLUS 2
## FREE GIFTS!

HARLEQUIN®

*Blaze*™

**Red-hot reads!**

---

HB09R3

**Stay up-to-date on all your romance-reading news with the brand-new Harlequin** *Inside Romance!*

The Harlequin *Inside Romance* is a **FREE** quarterly newsletter highlighting our upcoming series releases and promotions!

**Click on the *Inside Romance* link on the front page of www.eHarlequin.com or e-mail us at InsideRomance@Harlequin.ca to sign up to receive your FREE newsletter today!**

You can also subscribe by writing to us at: HARLEQUIN BOOKS
Attention: Customer Service Department
P.O. Box 9057, Buffalo, NY 14269-9057

*Please allow 4-6 weeks for delivery of the first issue by mail.*

IRNBPAQ309

# HARLEQUIN® *Blaze*™

## COMING NEXT MONTH

### Available November 24, 2009

**#507 BETTER NAUGHTY THAN NICE Vicki Lewis Thompson, Jill Shalvis, Rhonda Nelson**
*A Blazing Holiday Collection*
Bad boy Damon Claus is determined to mess things up for his jolly big brother, Santa. Who'd ever guess that sibling rivalry would result in mistletoe madness for three unsuspecting couples! And Damon didn't even have to spike the eggnog….

**#508 STARSTRUCK Julie Kenner**
For Alyssa Chambers, having the perfect Christmas means snaring the perfect man. And she has him all picked out. Too bad it's her best friend, Christopher Hyde, who has her seeing stars.

**#509 TEXAS BLAZE Debbi Rawlins**
*The Wrong Bed*
Hot and heavy. That's how Kate Manning and Mitch Colter have always been for each other. But it's not till Kate makes the right move—though technically in the wrong bed—that things start heating up for good!

**#510 SANTA, BABY Lisa Renee Jones**
*Dressed to Thrill, Bk. 4*
As a blonde bombshell, Caron Avery thinks she's got enough attitude to bring a man to his knees. But when she seduces hot playboy Baxter Remington, will she be the one begging for more?

**#511 CHRISTMAS MALE Cara Summers**
*Uniformly Hot!*
All policewoman Fiona Gallagher wants for Christmas is a little excitement. But once she finds herself working on a case with sexy captain D. C. Campbell, she's suddenly aching for a different kind of thrill….

**#512 TWELVE NIGHTS Hope Tarr**
*Blaze Historicals*
Lady Alys is desperately in love with Scottish bad boy Callum Fraser. And keeping him out of her bed until the wedding is nearly killing her. So what's stopping them from indulging? Uhh…Elys's deceased first husband, a man very much alive.

**www.eHarlequin.com**